advance praise for
ALL THE HOMETOWNS YOU CAN'T STAY AWAY FROM

"Izzy Wasserstein writes br[...]
change, and community—[...]
short work collected in this [...]
Hemlock. In *All the Hometou[...]*
Wasserstein explores trans and queer experiences in
semi-familiar landscapes—some of them Midwestern,
others unfolding in spaces and times far away. She has a
memorable literary voice, and her stories of alienation and
survival will haunt and sustain me for years to come."
—R.B. Lemberg, author of *The Four Profound Weaves*

"Izzy Wasserstein has a postapocalyptic sensibility. Her
debut collection *All the Hometowns You Can't Stay Away
From* contains many stories that deal with heart- and gut-
wrenching destruction and loss, but this makes the shards
of hope gleam all the brighter. Not everything is gone, and
some things worth fighting for still remain. Izzy Wasserstein
has an impressive range from epic fantasy to scientific
mystery, but the emotional core of these stories is invariably
resonant. *All the Hometowns You Can't Stay Away From* will
remain timely for the foreseeable future, and help guide
readers through moments of despair to hard-fought joy; it
belongs on your bookshelf too."
—Bogi Takács, author of *The Trans Space Octopus Congregation*

"Wasserstein's stories offer a finely-honed sense of place,
precise and evocative writing, and a beautiful, sometimes
chilling, exploration of what it means to be complicated and
human."
—Kate Elliott, author of *Unconquerable Sun*

Neon Hemlock Press
www.neonhemlock.com
@neonhemlock

All the Hometowns You Can't Stay Away From
Izzy Wasserstein

Cover Illustration by Vivian Magaña
Interior Illustrations by Vivian Magaña
Cover Design and Layout by dave ring

Print ISBN-13: 978-1-952086-42-7
Ebook ISBN-13: 978-1-952086-43-4

Izzy Wasserstein
ALL THE HOMETOWNS YOU CAN'T STAY AWAY FROM

Neon Hemlock Press

NEON HEMLOCK

All the Hometowns You Can't Stay Away From

BY IZZY WASSERSTEIN

in memory of Liz and Perry Wasserstein
who passed on their love of reading, dad jokes, and dogs

"We survive"
—Susan Jane Bigelow, "The Heart's Cartography"

"unbuild walls"
—Ursula K. Le Guin, *The Dispossessed*

stories

✹ I ✹

✹ II ✹

✹ III ✹

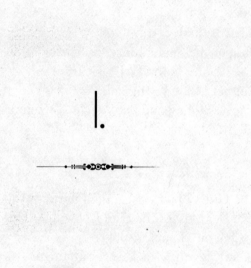

I.

All the
Hometowns
You Can't Stay
Away From

Y OU SNAP INTO the procedurally-generated shithole you call a hometown, and a moment later the stench leaves you gagging. So many universes and yet, in almost every one, South Topeka smells like a family of raccoons died inside a middle school locker room.

You tighten your travel bag around your shoulders, put your hands in your jacket pockets, and walk through the old neighborhood. The street signs don't quite match your memory—Kildare Street is Mayo, here—but the strip-mall is still half-abandoned, and the meth house on the corner still lacks all its windows. You stop outside the ranch house you grew up in, more or less, and stare at the front door for a long time. The siding has warped and the roof is in rough shape. The grass is high, half-hiding nasty clumps of sticker weeds. In one universe, you knocked and strangers peered at you from behind the deadbolt, and spoke in a language you hadn't heard in all your travels. But you're more afraid you will know the faces inside, so you hesitate.

(By "you hesitate," I mean I'm hesitating. We all do what we must to survive returning home. If I say you're the one doing this, maybe I'll believe things unfold as they must.)

Eventually you knock, because you want to get out of the reeking wind. Your brother opens the door and looks at you with such shock that you know that in this iteration you've not been around for a long time.

His hug is brittle. "Do you want to see mom?" he asks, but when you say yes he drives you to a cemetery. It was a mistake to come here. It always is.

Your room is waiting for you. You tell your brother you'll see him in the morning, wait until you're pretty sure he's asleep, then Snap out again. There's a simulated multiverse to see, but you promise yourself this is the last time some version of Topeka hauls you back. Still lying to yourself after all these years.

IN SO MANY realities, there are headstones carved with your mother's name. Sometimes your mother is buried under headstones with different names. And there are realities where she's still alive, and even ones where you never left.

In the ones where she's alive and you never left, the other yous seethe with resentment and jealousy, like you are a reminder of everything they don't have. You know just how they feel. In the ones where she's dead, the other yous have the look of cornered rats and you know all over again why you had to get out.

Sometimes you tell yourself you are looking for the right reality, maybe one where you made peace and she died holding your hand. Or one where she screamed at you until you knew leaving was right. Or maybe she got better and you went off to college and this is your triumphant return. In one reality, your sibling (your sister, this time) explains the paradox of choice: choosing between three salad dressings is easy; choosing between one hundred, a nightmare.

"Narrow your choices," she tells you, somewhere into the second bottle of bottom-shelf whiskey. "Settle for good enough."

In that Topeka, your mother is dead and so is that version of you. Your sister doesn't ask to come with you.

◊

YOU'RE STANDING ON the street looking at your mother's house when another you steps out the front door. Her hair is still its natural brown, and she's maybe five years older than you, but she has the same scar across her cheek, the same beat-up travel bag. She sees you, sighs, and shakes her head, wordlessly telling you not to bother going inside. Later, the two of you break into the old State Hospital building, and smoke weed the way you both used to do with friends when you were sixteen, before you left. You compare notes.

"I've been out a long way," she says. "Way past the 'human life' cluster."

You admit you've never dared go out that far. "What is it like out there?"

"Different kinds of life, and in some universes you can't survive and have to Snap out right away. Once I was almost crushed by the gravity in the moments it took me to Snap."

"Do you think the level above us is real?" you ask, because you're high. The math is pretty simple: once a universe can make a simulated universe, it can make many. Any universe simulated well enough can make its own simulations. There might be infinite simulated universes for every real one.

"I don't know why I would care," she says. "Can't get there and, even if I could, why would 'real' mean anything to me?"

"Oh." You sit with this a minute. "Do you ever think about going back to your original reality?"

She looks at you with pity that feels like a knife's edge. "Don't try it," she says. "Trust me. Don't."

"You don't want to know the truth?" you ask her and, because you're high, you don't realize until much later that isn't what she meant at all.

"You'll go crazy looking for those kind of answers, kid," she says. You've always hated being called "kid," and it's harder to take advice from yourself than you expected.

"You came back here, too, bitch," you tell her.

She's quiet for a long time. "Yeah," she says. "I can't seem to stop myself."

After that there's nothing to say, and soon you Snap out.

THERE ARE A sizable minority of iterations, like yours, where people know their reality is a simulation. In some of those simulations, people figure out how to Snap to other universes. Not as many leave as one might expect, though. Knowing reality is simulated doesn't change much for most people, maybe influences their religion a little. You can talk about holograms all you want, but chemo still wrecks the body, or some other treatment does, and there are still words that can never be unsaid. Everyone hurts in every universe, and the ones who leave find new ways to hurt.

In all probability, there are universes out there where these things aren't true. Simulations where life never evolves, maybe even ones where it doesn't suffer, though you find that hard to imagine. If you wanted to travel far enough from your cluster of simulations, maybe you could find them. Instead, you stick to the ones where Earth exists, and in more or less the same human-fucked configurations. You tell yourself this is because it's safer, but in truth it's just something to hang on to.

SOMETIMES YOU TAKE a lover to Topeka. Once you took two. Some versions of your mother adore your paramours, and some hate them. It doesn't change anything. You don't seem capable of staying with anyone for more than a few Snaps.

"Still ghosting everyone?" one sibling asks you, and the woman you've brought with you pretends not to hear. For the first time, you wonder how many times versions of you have visited this family, what it must be like to have different yous stopping by to work out your shit. You don't stay long.

IN THE REALITY you were born to (indicated by an impossibly-long series of coordinates on the Snapper strapped to your wrist) it starts like this. It's mid-afternoon and you stumble into your mother's hospital room, a little drunk and a lot angry. You half-hoped she'd be asleep, but she's awake and alert, even though she's lost so much weight that she looks like a half-formed copy of herself.

"You're drunk," she says.

"No," you lie, and you go on because some part of you wants to burn everything down. "Last night I was drunk. Now I'm just hungover."

A sound behind you, your brother in the doorway, holding a juice-box and staring. He's twelve years old and wants nothing so much as for you not to fight.

"I can't believe I raised a stupid girl," your mother says. "Out half the night, drunk, in this town? Don't you know what could happen to you?"

You know, as it happens. Just like you know someone can turn to religion at nineteen, become a teetotaler, like she did, and still get cancer in their mid-thirties.

"I don't care," you tell her. "I'm allowed to have a good time."

Your mother looks at you with contempt that would have withered you only a few months ago. But now you're sixteen, and she's a dying woman, and you think you hate her more than anything. "You think a good time makes any difference? When it comes time to integrate with Jesus, you gonna talk about a 'good time'?"

You're drunk and already looking for a way out, so you say, "Shut up about Jesus! What the fuck has he ever done for us?"

That's about when the screaming starts, when your brother runs out of the room, and later you wonder whether what hurt your mother the most was your rejection of her faith, or that you would take away the one thing she was still hanging on to.

That night you steal a Snapper, telling yourself the man dying a few doors down from your mother won't need it, and shortly after that you are in another universe, swearing you won't come back. You were lying to yourself right from the start.

ONCE YOU FOUND a Topeka to which one of you returned, and everyone seemed to get along. The you that has settled there glared at you over the dinner table, kissed her mother on the forehead, and set to cleaning up the dishes. You wanted to tell her that you weren't angling to steal the life she's made. Instead you stepped outside to smoke and Snapped before you had to say anything at all.

YOU'VE BECOME SUCH an expert at leaving that you aren't prepared for it when you get left (xe had eyes like ice caves, and hands to make your body ache in all the best ways). You make a lot of bad choices in a handful of realities and, as you always do when you're being self-destructive, you start thinking it's time to visit Topeka again. You dial up your original universe for the first time. You tell yourself it's time to face the grave of your mother, or her survival, at last.

You're still telling yourself that when a man you don't recognize opens the door and calls you by name. Your father, the piece of shit who ran before you were old enough to have memories of him, but somehow he's been here all along. He stares at you in horror, because his daughter has been dead for many years.

Neither one of you can stand to make eye contact. You should be back home, but you aren't, and you don't have any answers for him or yourself. You Snap out before you can ask about your mother.

◊

YOU DON'T KNOW what went wrong, so you stay away from Topekas for a long time. There are infinite things to see, so for a while you are content. You travel with a physicist. Neither of you wants sex from the other but, as the nights get longer, both of you need the heat of each other to help you sleep.

One night you tell her about your trip home, to your original home, and she strokes your hair and whispers how sorry she is.

"You can't just remove part of the simulation," she tells you. "When you leave a universe, or when you enter one, it changes it. Permanently. The whole of it iterates."

She talks about quantum effects, non-linearity and software glitches, and you don't follow it. You're thinking of the universe that ceased to be the moment you left it behind.

For a long time after that you can't Snap. Maybe the thing to do is to stay where you are, since you can't know what changing realities will do to either one. This universe seems no worse than any other. The physicist doesn't share your concerns.

"You'll change the world by staying, too," she says. "No reason to get sentimental about it." You don't have anything to say to each other after that, and soon she is on to the next universe, and just as the nights are at their coldest.

You travel slowly back towards your hometown, catching buses when you can and hitchhiking when you can't. You still can't settle for the safe life. A truck driver drops you off at the tollbooth, and your lungs fill with the stench in the air. It is after midnight and the streetlights stand like specters against the fog. You hesitate. If you keep going, if you knock on that door, you'll find answers. A set of answers, anyway. Your hands twist into fists.

Each simulation functions as an equation: plug yourself in or take yourself out. All those homes you left, they exist only in your memory, now. Do you make new worlds or make yourself part of this one?

You walk through the streets, Kilkenny, Clare, Mayo, trying to decide, until your house emerges from the darkness like a familiar face.

Their Eyes Like
Dead Lamps

I SAW THE car coming from a long way off, first as a
line of dust up along the ridge, then bending its way
forward, disappearing and reappearing behind the
hills. A black sedan, gleaming in the late afternoon sun,
the kind of car only city people owned, all but useless in
the winter. Most people along the banks of the Marais
des Cygnes River had trucks, and the cars you saw were
old and rusted and not bothered about the dirt that caked
their sides. This car had the look of people who bothered.

"Some big shot," I said. Cassie frowned. Her shoulders
tensed. "I'll see what's up. You want to wait in the cellar?"

"I guess so," she said, looking relieved I'd suggested
it. She pulled aside the rug at the base of my fort and
together we yanked open the wooden door. She grabbed
her flashlight and dropped away into the darkness. I
closed the door and covered it back up. The place had
been a root cellar for someone, long ago, and now we were
the only two people in the world who knew it existed.

The car stopped in front of my house and a man
and woman walked up to the front porch, the way
visitors would when they didn't know us well enough to

understand everyone came and went through the kitchen. Momma must have been watching, because she stepped out on the porch to meet them. Before long the three of them were coming this way.

I busied myself with my sketchbook in case anyone peeked in, but Momma knocked and I clambered out through the narrow door.

"Moira," she said, her forehead wrinkled, "these folks are from the government. They're looking for Cassie."

I sized up the visitors. The man was wearing slacks and a white dress shirt already half sweated through, though it was a pleasant enough July day, and the woman stood uneasily on a pair of low heels that were still no match for the soft, gopher-infested stretch of yard between the house and my fort.

"Ain't seen her," I said, "all day."

The two strangers glanced at each other, and Momma frowned.

"It's very important," the lady said. She knelt beside me and used the voice adults did when they thought kids were idiots. "We're here to help her, but we can't do that if we can't find her." Even then, ten years old, I knew how much you could rely on adults' help.

"If I see her, I'll tell her that," I said.

"You don't mind if I poke my head in?" Momma asked, and then I knew it was serious.

"Suit yourself," I said, one of her favorite phrases. She knelt and stuck her head through the opening. The fort wasn't much, really, a single room built of discarded wood and metal, littered with dolls and action figures, sketchbooks and pencils, old junk hauled from rummage sales and abandoned houses. The kind of stuff that gathers to people with lots more time than money.

No Cassie, of course.

"You're sure you ain't seen her?" Momma asked.

"Not all day," I said.

When the people's car had started back up the hill, Momma went back inside and I pulled aside the door and dropped down into the root cellar. The previous summer, we'd hauled down a plastic table and some chairs and set them in the center, surrounded by the sagging shelves and the ancient preserves rotting in darkness. A great place, we agreed, for a tea party or ghost stories. Cassie was sitting at the table, blinking at the sudden intrusion of light.

"They're gone back up the hill," I told her.

She brushed cobwebs from her hair and smiled. "Thanks."

I didn't ask her what was going on, wouldn't have considered it. Not any more than she'd have asked me about where my father was. Something about the prairie builds that kind of reserve. Maybe it's the wind.

"Momma won't be watching once I come in for dinner," I told her. Then it would be easy for her to sneak off. The house stood between us and the river, but this close to water the land was thick with trees, and we'd built the fort along a windbreak that someone had planted decades before. You could sneak along those trees, back up to the road, dart across it and be on her property in a few minutes. No one would see you if you didn't want them to. We were experts at being unseen.

"Yeah." She was looking down past the house, where the river was a band of silver in the late afternoon sun. "Someday, the River Riders will come for me."

It wasn't the first time she'd said that. It seemed like every kid at school had a story about the Riders, or the Bloody Widow of Miami County. My grandmother liked to tell of Sidhe nobles who had traveled with her people across the Atlantic.

"YOU AIN'T SEEN Cassie?" Momma asked at dinner. Her forehead was still creased and I figured I might be in trouble.

"Yesterday," I said, not quite meeting her eyes. Spam sandwiches with fresh tomatoes. My favorite.

"If you do see her, you tell me right away, you hear? Nobody's seen her father in a while, and someone needs to look out for her."

I didn't know how adults decided which disappearances were part of the natural way of things, like my father running off, and which were a problem. But now I knew which one they thought about Cassie's father. When Momma wasn't looking, I put half my sandwich in my lap. Cassie would be hungry in the morning.

"YOU REALLY THINK the River Riders will come for you?" I asked Cassie the next day. We were playing in the muddy banks half a mile from my house, just us, the cattails, the shade of overhanging trees. Overhead, a Prairie Falcon circled.

She looked at me strangely, pausing from her half-finished mud-castle. The river had been running high and fast all summer, and the banks were thick with mud that I tracked everywhere, much to Momma's annoyance.

"I dunno," she said, and was silent for a while before she went on. "I figure they watch the river. Or maybe they just ride down it, sometimes. They'll come around sometimes for a few weeks, or just a night or two, and then I won't see them for awhile."

"Like carnival people?" This I knew something about.

She shrugged. "Yeah, maybe. Something like that. Do you want to go swimming?"

I didn't see Cassie the next day, or the day after. Momma asked me about her, and I didn't have to lie. Usually she'd have called me if she couldn't play, but if she did that, Momma would know she had, and then the government people would know too and would hurry down from Osawatomie or even Kansas City.

The third day, when she wasn't waiting for me at my fort, I grabbed a bag of chocolate-chip cookies and went over to her place. We preferred the privacy of the fort, but then, if her father wasn't around, we'd have privacy at her place, too. It was no more than a mile from ours, over the old rail bridge that stayed open even when the river flooded. Her father's property wasn't much, a run-down shotgun house about two steps from abandoned, tucked between the sweep of the river and the low hills. His rusted-out Ford was sitting on blocks in the front yard, and for a moment I hesitated to knock.

When no one answered I pushed open the screen door and slipped inside, but there was just the usual piles of newspapers, auto parts, stacks of green-and-brown bottles, paper bags filled with who-knows-what, shards of pottery on strings dangling from the ceiling, clacking together as an old fan rotated back and forth across the invisible line where the living room and kitchen merged. The place smelled of damp and mold.

I'd never liked it in there, and I ducked back out and made my way down to the river. That's where I spotted her, kneeling beside the bank, the water moving swiftly beyond her. I started to call her name, but it caught in my throat. Two shapes were beside her on the bank, obscured by the tall grass between us, and by the bright sunlight off the river. They were maybe half her size, with heads that reminded me of water moccasins and long, sinuous limbs. I stood, I don't know for how long, perhaps fifty yards from her.

Then a car backfired up the road, and I turned in surprise. When I looked back, she was alone, coming up the river toward me.

I smiled and waved, but there was a closed look to her face, the kind I knew, the kind Momma had when she told me it was just the two of us, now. Maybe I was afraid. Maybe my concern for my only friend outweighed my curiosity. Maybe it was just that I couldn't escape the feeling we were being watched.

"I brought cookies," I said, and she smiled.

IF ALL THIS had happened two years earlier, I'd have accepted it easily. But the world starts to narrow, and by the time someone—your mother or your aunt or whoever—sits you down for The Talk, everything has calcified. If I'd been younger, I would probably remember all this as play, or as a trick my mind played to cover for what really happened. If I'd been older, maybe I wouldn't have seen anything down by the bank besides Cassie.

That night I lay in bed, listening to the thunderstorm that swept in, as they often did, from the south and west, and thinking of those shapes along the bank, imagining sharp teeth, eyes like dead lamps. No one ever built a fort because the world was safe.

CASSIE WAS WAITING for me in the fort the next morning. She was curled up in my sleeping bag, reading. Maybe she'd been there all night. Sometimes she was, when her father was angry or gone.

"Mornin'," I said, and handed her a box of Pop Tarts. I'm not sure how I knew she was hungry all the time.

I don't remember her ever complaining about it.

"Good mornin'." She tore open the package and ate ravenously. She was wearing the same dress as yesterday, blue and green swirls, its hem ragged and muddy. I looked down at my jeans, faded but clean. When she was done, we talked about what we were going to do with the day. Cassie wanted to go to the brambles a ways down the river and pick blackberries. But that wasn't what I wanted.

"Can I see them, Cassie?"

She scrunched her face up. "See who?"

"You know. Them. The River Riders."

"They won't talk to you."

This felt like betrayal. "Why not?"

She looked at me with something like pity, which even then I couldn't stand.

She pressed her hand over mine. "Don't feel bad, Moira." Her voice was barely more than a whisper. "They don't make friends."

"But you're their friend."

"No," she said sadly. "I'm not. I'm just someone they— feel obliged to."

"Obliged? For what?"

"Way back, my mom helped them." She'd never talked about her mother before. "There was some problem they had, upriver. One night she took the truck and was out all night. Next day, she was real quiet. Since she left, the Riders check up on me, sometimes." She looked away. Above us, a raven chattered. "I want blackberries," she said.

We snuck through the Harrises' fence and ate blackberries until I felt sick, then came away with our hands and mouths stained deep purple. She would tell me no more about the River Riders. The first big secret between us, unless you counted all the things we knew about the adult world that we never said. All the way back along the river's edge, I thought I felt eyes on us. But I saw nothing besides a swarm of starlings pecking at the ground.

I saw the cars in the driveway a long way off. Two of them, one flashing red and blue lights. Cassie had frozen at the top of the rise. She looked at me, wide-eyed, then crouched down in the tall grass.

"I should go home," she said.

"They'll be there, too." I'd never seen her look so helpless. "I'll go talk to them. You sneak to the fort and hide below. It will take a while, because Momma will be on the lookout, but I'll come get you when it's clear."

She set her jaw fiercely. "Okay," she said, and then, as if to reassure herself, "Okay."

We made our way down toward my house. At the windbreak we separated. I saw Cassie moving among the trees, hunched over, and then she was gone. I stood up straight and walked home.

Momma was waiting on the porch, and in the living room were two cops and the government people. They sat me down, asked if I'd seen Cassie. I hadn't.

"This is very serious," Momma said. "These nice men need to find Cassie right away."

The government man put his hand on my shoulder. I jumped, and he pulled it back. "It's about her father, Moira," he said. His voice was a low rumble. I looked to Momma, and saw everything in her expression.

"He's dead," I said. Mom knelt and hugged me, and I felt the adults shifting uneasily behind her.

"Yes, honey," she whispered.

"I don't know where she is," I said after a while, wiping at my eyes.

"You weren't playing with her today?" Momma asked.

"I wanted to, but she never showed up."

I could see she didn't believe me.

The cops' radio squawked, and one stepped out onto the porch. When he returned he shook his head. Momma understood him. "Cassie needs your help, Moira. Where would she go?"

I looked at my toes and thought hard.

"Would you excuse us for a moment?" Momma asked the adults, and after a few moments they went outside.

"Moira," Momma said, gently touching my cheek. "This isn't like when you help her hide from the school people. We need to help her."

"Momma, I—I can't." My voice quavered; the uncertainty behind my words hung in the air.

"You have to, darling. Please."

Momma's gaze held me.

"The fort," I said. Momma took my hand and we went out to the others together. She told them quietly. We all trudged out to the fort in the gathering darkness. They crouched and peered inside, but there was nothing to see. I thought of Cassie in her fraying clothes, of the desperate way she devoured sweets. I thought of her roaming freely long past my bedtime, of the deals her people had made with the River Riders from which I was forever excluded. I could feel myself caught between ugliness and ugliness, a feeling I've since come to know well. I buried my face against my mother's side and told them about the cellar.

I couldn't watch them as they pulled apart one wall of the fort and forced their way down into the cellar. My eyes were burning, and I kept pressed to Momma. I couldn't face Cassie.

But when they came up the silence lingered, and finally Momma said, "Where else could she be, Moira?"

I looked up at the worried faces, then rushed past them, through the open door. Nothing but roots and old junk and our plastic table in the dirt. No Cassie. Never again.

❧

THEY LOOKED FOR weeks, but I stopped my search the next morning. Down by the river in the fresh mud was one footprint, the worn sole of Cassie's boot. And beside it, two strange points, each like a malformed star. The hair on my neck stood up, but look as closely as I might I saw no eyes watching me. The river swept past, down toward the Osage.

A few days later I built up the courage to go back to her house, but there was no one there. She had taken nothing from her cramped room. One wall sagged. The others were lined with my sketches.

For a while I'd see her "missing" poster at the Post Office or on lightposts when we'd drive into Osawatomie. And then they were gone too.

That was the last summer I'd be free to do what I wanted. When school started in the fall, Momma insisted I trade my pants for dresses, and when the next summer rolled around, she made sure I had plenty to keep me busy, too busy to go running around unattended. Of course, she had good reason, and on my own it wouldn't have been the same, anyway.

And that's the end of it. Almost the end. When I left for college, I thought I had left the river behind me for good. But one rainy summer I drove home to visit Momma, and found a package waiting for me beside the back door, a small box wrapped in brown paper and bound with twine. No return address, no postage, just my name, scrawled in a hand I thought I recognized. Inside was a package of strange cookies, wrapped in delicate paper the colors of a Kansas sunset, and etched with words in no language I knew.

I went out to the treeline. I had never rebuilt the fort, but the decayed cellar door opened for me. I knelt beside the dirt-clotted table. In the twilight of that cellar, I tore open the package. The cookies were a swirl of colors, blue and brown and silver, like the different faces of the river.

They smelled like the air after a storm, and tasted of sugar and blackberries. I ate the whole bag, slowly.

Unplaces:
An Atlas of
Non-Existence

*E*xcerpts from the First Edition, with handwritten
marginalia. Recovered from the ruins of Kansas City.
Part of the permanent exhibit of the Museum of Fascisms.

Section 1: Places that Never Were

Avalon: Island home of the legendary sword Excalibur,
attested to in *Historia regum Britanniae*. A land which
produces all good things, Avalon has been claimed to
be synonymous with various historical places, including
Glastonbury, England, and Avallon, Burgundy. Smythe
and Bliss (2018) claim this island once existed, but it is
more probable that it is symbolic of a general longing for a
better land beyond one's own.

[Lya: I had this book on loan from the Spencer Library
when the Messianic Army reached Lawrence. After
OKC, I knew they'd soon burn the collection. My beloved
books are all gone, along with my years of research on lost

places. The only book I was able to save isn't even mine, and now I'm reduced to defacing it. Forgive me. I write these words out of hope that they will reach you, and out of faith that our words still matter.]

El Dorado: The "city of gold" legend evolved from older stories of a golden prince, and was whispered to European conquerors desperate for riches. There is no evidence of the city's existence, and the search for it certainly destroyed many other places, both real and once-real. As with many Unplaces, historical fact is obscured by conquerors eager to make their own history. In so doing they efface the past.

[When I was a student—just months ago, though it seems much longer—these entries were mostly of academic interest to me, I'm ashamed to admit. Now they mean something more each day. Who wouldn't send the Conquistadors away on a hunt for gold, if they could? Last we heard, most of the world—even most of Europe—was free from the fascists. Maybe it's just the Americas that are fucked. Maybe the places that lack our particular combination of Authoritarianism and apocalyptic faith will overcome.

I'd like to believe I'd never inflict this horror on someone else to save myself. But to see you again, Lya? All things are compromised—our world, our home, myself.]

Erșetu la târi: Attested to throughout ancient Mesopotamia as the land of the dead. One reached it by going through seven gates, and at each gate left behind an article of clothing, so that one arrived in the next life naked, a kind of un-birth. Szymborska (2020) argues that Erșetu la târi may have once existed, given widespread belief in it. If so, however, there can be no evidence of its existence, for its name translates to "earth of no return."

[I want to leave Kansas City, to flee to someplace safer. But even if I was sure where to go, how would I get there?

It's not even safe to scavenge for food uptown.

I'm fortunate that the militias mostly stay out of the old downtown, the areas that were never redeveloped. They may catch me even here, but I am as careful as my desperation allows. I stay in old brick buildings, long-abandoned warehouses, with clear views and multiple exits. There's been no wealth in these neighborhoods for generations, and the militias prefer to root out subversives in areas they can loot.

Nevertheless, at night every creak and groan of the old buildings fills me with dread. If I am found, if this book is lost, these forgotten spaces will be my Erșetu la târi.]

Kyöpelinvuori: From the Finnish for "ghost mountain," a place haunted by dead women. Some scholars argue it once existed, either predating Christianity in the region, or perhaps coming into existence as local gods were displaced by the arrival of new ones. Linna (2021) argues that dead women haunt liminal spaces in every culture. They exist where they can, and those who are silenced in life often speak in death.

[Last night I dreamed I was a ghost, screaming because they'd found me at last. I woke fearing this book was my scream.]

Leng, Plateau of: Antarctic Plateau colonized by Elder Things in the works of H. P. Lovecraft. When cultists successfully raised R'lyeh from what had been an empty seabed, expeditions were mounted to see if Leng had also been brought into existence. No evidence was forthcoming. "Our horrors are closer to home," as Coates remarked.

[Lovecraft panicked over people of color, immigrants, imagined them as murderous or worse. He should've worried about a different kind of cultist. A bunch of white kids slavering over Lovecraft's statue brought R'lyeh back.

I wonder how many of those kids march through the streets of North American cities now, in uniform? Having failed to end the world, have they settled for effacing it?

I found a radio last week, and there are pirate stations, rebel stations. They urge us to hold onto hope, but they don't report much good news. I do not know how to fight this evil. I write instead.]

Zerzura: "The Oasis of Little Birds," a white-walled city in the Sahara, guarded by giants. Attested to in Arabic texts since the 13th century CE, and possibly predating Herodotus. Farouk (2019) demonstrates that all extant references to the city are from foreigners, and that no local tales reference it. Thus the most likely origin of the Zerzura story is a combination of colonizers' fears and hallucinations. Note that modern European interest in the city predates Imaginary Anthropology and so is unlikely to have made Zerzura real.

[The militias swept the area today; I braced myself in the frames of the wall between floors, and managed to escape. This time.

Fires spread across the skyline. I grow more desperate to leave. There is nowhere to go. I'd hoped, in saving this book, to find some insight that might help me, some way out, even if it is into unreality. Nothing.]

Section 2: Places that Once Existed

Azeb: From the Hebrew for "leave behind, forsake, abandon." Shown by Lee (2020) to be the place where lost objects gathered. Some have argued that it is synonymous with various cities of the dead, but loss and death have never been equivalent. Many documented methods of entering Azeb exist, though few exits have been found. There have been no verified reports of accessible entrances since at least 2017. It is likely, though not certain, that Azeb itself is forever lost to us.

[I had a friend who went searching for Azeb. Never heard from her again. I knew ways in, of course: what scholar of lost things wouldn't? Yesterday I tried to open a path, using the reflection of a full moon on still water, my own blood, and the second most valuable thing I own: a pair of dry socks. The way is closed. Seems I'll meet my fate here, Lya, less than a mile from the last place it was safe for us to walk holding hands.]

Cimmeria: The first triumph of Imaginary Anthropology (Goss, 2014), now lost due to conflict in the region and active condemnation of the discipline by foreign-backed warlords (may this book keep Cimmeria's memory alive, though this author was unable to keep it from joining the other Unplaces. Some nights, she can still smell the bazaar).

[I'm crying as I write this. Cimmeria's lost forever, and we never walked its streets. So much has been lost, and now even history is being erased. Then they'll make a new past, written in blood and marches and violent slogans and there will be nothing left.]

Penglai: Once a mountain on an island in the eastern Bohai Sea, attested by some sources to be home to the Immortals. Penglai was a land of abundance, with fruit that could cure any disease. Demonstrated by Kusano (2017) to have once existed, it was lost no later than the 2nd century BCE, when Qin Shi Huang dispatched expeditions seeking the elixir of life that failed to locate it.

[Lying awake last night, listening to gunfire in the distance, I wondered about the last person to set foot on Penglai. Did they know the paradise on which they

walked would soon be gone forever? Did they treasure
its memory? When they died, did Penglai die with them?
I'm trying to hold on, Lya, but I feel everything slipping
away.]

Tlön: A parallel world to Earth, probably first brought
into existence in the 19th century CE. Known to be
definitively real by 1940 CE. In Tlön, only those things
exist which are observed, and there is no deity to do the
observing. For reasons which are still debated, this world
was lost to us, apparently forever, with the use of the
Bomb over Hiroshima.

[In Tlön, a ruin might disappear from existence if there
was not, say, a fox or a disinterested snake to observe it.
The past is only as secure as our memory of it.

When they find me, or I starve, or die in a fire, will
this book survive? Will it serve as a memory? Or will
everything that I remember die with me?

I hope you got out, Lya. I hope that "out" is a place
that still exists. If you did, remember. Remember. I'll do
the same. It's all that is left to me. Goodbye, goodbye.]

[I thought I couldn't go on. I thought I was done with
words. Then you appeared to me—a dream, a vision, a
fevered hallucination?—and whispered in my ear that
this book is incomplete. You were right. And so, as the sun
rises over the burned-out city, I add a new entry:

PLACES THAT MIGHT YET BE:

Matsa: From the Hebrew "to find, to attain," Matsa
waits for those who reject utopias, who believe we are
doomed if we allow the mistakes of the past to overtake us.

Matsa will be a place and a journey. We make it real only by seeking it out.

In Matsa, we will not forgive the fascists. We will light flames for the dead, and we will train ourselves against forgetting. When they try to burn our books, to make our places into Unplaces, we will, each of us, carry the past with us.

If you find this book, make Matsa real. I will await you. Yours Always,
Hannah]

The Museum thanks Dr. Lya Carew for the generous gift of this book. Dr. Carew asks that those wishing to honor the memory of Hannah Leibowitz make donations to the Free Lawrence Library's Matsa reconstructive history project.

The Good
Mothers' Home for
Wayward Girls

O NE OF THE Mothers shoves the new girl into the
dorm room, the slick threads of the Mother's
grasp lingering long enough that several of us
shiver. The new girl wears a short dress, shot through
with sunset, though we are not sure we remember sunsets
properly. The hem of the dress is ragged and mud-caked.
It is the most beautiful thing we have ever seen. We hate
the new girl.

Get her into uniform, the Mother commands. It makes
no sound, but its words echo between our ears. The
new girl has been standing with her hands on opposite
shoulders, her chin jutting forward. That changes when
we surround her. We rip the dress from her shoulders
and toss a gray shift over her body. Now she is dressed
just as we are.

The Mother squelches out of the room, and the door
slams shut behind it.

The new girl is skinny, Kate says. Kate hates the new
girl more than the rest of us, and is far more relieved that
she has arrived.

Too skinny, Miranda agrees. You think you're pretty, new girl? Miranda has been at the Good Mothers' Home the longest of any of us. She has not been the new girl in a very long time, but she is not inclined to mercy.

My name is Bel, the new girl says.

No one cares, new girl. Kate shoves her. The new girl stumbles back, then raises her fists. There is something in her eyes we recognize. Not all new girls have it. Kate, who was the new girl for a long time, did not have it. Kate is caught, now, picking a fight with someone who will not cower like she once did.

Say that again, the new girl demands. Kate hesitates.

The great clock in the hallway strikes NIGHT. A Mother outside the door forces a word in our heads: *Bed.* We scramble into our bunks. The gas lamps flicker and die. The new girl does not move.

Bed. The voice in our heads is louder the second time. It feels like a rat scratching behind our eyes.

Get in bed, new girl, we shout, and Jaq cracks her knuckles. The new girl gets into bed, and the Mother's pressure in our minds fades.

Kate says: If you get us in trouble, new girl, you'll pay. We'll make you pay. Kate has scars down her back that were not there when she arrived.

When she thinks the rest of us are asleep, Molly tiptoes over to the new girl's bed. Welcome to The Home, new girl, she says. The new girl does not respond. We fall asleep wondering if we hear scratching and scraping noises outside.

IN THE MORNING—that is, when the gas lamps ignite—the new girl's dress, which we left on the floor, is gone. We shuffle down to the bathroom. No one bothers to tell the

new girl what is happening. She doesn't ask. Kate hangs
back and stage-whispers: You're not going to survive, new
girl. The Mothers will punish you or you'll slit your wrists.
Kate is brave because there are Mothers watching us, one
in the doorway to the kitchen, one clinging to the ceiling,
leaving a puddle of ichor on the moldy tile of the hall. We
will need to clean up that mess later.

No. We will make the new girl do it.

A Mother oversees us in the bathroom, its undulating
form sliding like a misplaced shadow out of the corner.
We do not understand the Mothers, but we know some
things they hate, like fights and uncleanliness. This means
Kate cannot hurt the new girl the way she would like (we
can feel the ache coming off her like heat from the ruin
of her back). But she can still use words. Skinny, she says.
Look at those ribs. We join in, because we hate the new
girl. The new girl does not cry, though her face reddens.
We remember that she did not scream when the Mother
touched her.

We leave the bathroom. The great clock reads DAY,
but the light that spills in from the windows high above
us does not look like what we remember of daylight. We
doubt Miranda remembers daylight at all. Now we mark
time like this: when the clock strikes NIGHT, we hide in
our dorm until DAY returns and the lamps ignite. Some
of us remember a girl who snuck out at night. We cannot
forget her screams.

We eat breakfast at the long table in the dining hall.
The porridge is slightly bitter, which Jaq prefers to bland,
but Molly retches at the taste. When the new girl goes
to take a bite, Kate knocks her bowl away. There are no
Mothers watching, no one to punish her.

The new girl stands up. She is shorter than Kate and
lighter, but even Jaq tenses. Kate's eye widen but she does
not stand.

Let's settle this, the new girl says. We don't know where

the fierceness in her comes from. Were we ever like that? we wonder, and then hate her more for making us ask.

Kate looks down at the chipped tabletop. The new girl grabs her porridge and sits down.

After breakfast, we do our chores. *Chores build character*, the Mothers remind us often. *We will refine you*. We scrub floors that never come clean, whitewash peeling wallpaper, prune the gray-leafed trees in the enclosed garden. Over time, we have cleaned the whole of the Home, the dorm room, the dining hall, the kitchen, the bathroom. There is so much to clean. Miranda thinks there used to be many more Wayward Girls, because there are so many empty bunks, so much empty space. But we cannot be sure.

You're cleaning up after the Mothers, new girl, Miranda says.

I am not, says the new girl. She plants her feet and crosses her arms.

Do it, Kate says, or we'll hurt you.

Shut up, Kate, Miranda says. New girl, clean it or we'll make sure it costs you. Show her your back, Kate.

Kate cringes. Her shoulders hunch. I don't want to, she says.

Do it now, Miranda says.

Kate's gaze is a well of bitterness. She turns and lifts the rough fabric over her head. The new girl looks.

The Mothers will do worse than that, Molly says. She was not the new girl for long, and still has some sympathy left. The new girl stands very still. Then she grabs a pail and sets to work.

On her second night, the new girl takes a piece of broken glass and makes two scratches on the wall above her bed. We loudly take bets on how long she will keep that up.

That night we are almost sure we hear a snuffling outside the walls of The Home.

THE NEW GIRL has made many, many scratches by the morning of the fight. Kate has stopped trying to fight the new girl, because Kate is a coward. That is why we hated her for so long, we tell ourselves. Only Molly doesn't hate Kate, because Kate became the new girl so soon after Molly.

Kate does not want to fight the new girl, but she wants her to bleed. The new girl talks about feeling the wind blow across her arms, and about the tang of sourdough between her lips. She talks about the smell of the sea, the feeling of gravel between her toes. Kate hates her, and grows clever in her desire to hurt. She waits for Jaq to have a bad day. And Jaq does when a Mother spreads its ichor all over the garden and makes Jaq clean it.

We never know why the Mothers do what they do. Miranda once told us that, long ago, a girl asked, and a Mother said *For your protection, sweet thing,* and wrapped its appendages around the girl. After that, the girl didn't ask any more questions. She just stood, slack-mouthed, drooling.

This time the Mother makes Jaq clean the garden for so long she is late for dinner, rushing to fill her plate before it is too late, before we are shepherded to the dorm, before the clock strikes NIGHT.

Kate waits until Jaq is walking to the table with her tray, then shoves the new girl backwards off the bench and into Jaq. The porridge spills everywhere. The new girl struggles to her feet and turns to Kate, eyes burning with hate. But Jaq stands almost as fast and she tackles the new girl.

They scramble on the floor. The new girl is clever and vicious. She jabs her thumbs at Jaq's eyes, bites and claws. But Jaq is much stronger, and thinks she used to be a fighter, before the Mothers took her in. And she is covered in ichor.

Jaq has so much rage. It is frightening to watch. Even Kate looks away.

We see the Mother coming, but Jaq does not hear our hissed warnings.

Enough, the mother says. The word rattles our skulls in its fury. Jaq freezes and stands up. The ichor that pools beneath her is streaked with blood. Jaq shakes. The Mother will discipline her, perhaps take her away forever. It has happened before.

Look at this mess, the mother says. Kate bursts into sobs.

Somehow, the new girl is on her feet. She braces herself against the table. She is bleeding from her lip, from her nose, from a dozen cuts. Her eye is already swelling.

Tell me, the Mother orders.

Tell you what? the new girl asks. Molly gasps.

Tell me what she has done, the Mother says, and its oily appendage taps Jaq on the forehead, leaving a further smear on her brow. Jaq cowers.

We fell, the new girl says. It's nothing.

We stare at her, our mouths hanging open.

Do not lie to me, girl, the Mother says. *It is unbecoming.* It draws the last word out until it echoes between our ears. Molly claws at the skin on her arms.

It was an accident, the new girl says.

The Mother slides very close to her. It reeks of honey and rotted meat. The new girl is shaking. The new girl does not look away. *You must both be corrected*, the Mother says.

TWO DAYS LATER, a Mother shoves Bel and Jaq back into the dorm. Bel's wounds have not healed. The two girls are holding hands. They remind us of ships that have broken against a reef. They do not meet our eyes. We are very quiet.

The clock strikes. The lights burn out. In the darkness, we hear Jaq climb into Bel's bed. In moments, they are asleep in one another's arms.

In the morning, Bel asks how long it has been. When we tell her, she makes the marks on the wall above her head. Afterwards, she stares at the shard of glass for a long time. Jaq stares at her.

That night we are listening for the clock when Bel, perched on the end of her bunk, says, Why do we do what they say?

Shut up, new girl, Kate says.

You shut up, Jaq says, and Kate flinches.

Because they will hurt us, Miranda says.

Or kill us, Molly says.

Because of the things outside, Jaq says, very softly. Everyone goes quiet, but it is not yet NIGHT, and there are no sounds beyond the walls.

Death would be better than this, Bel says.

Would it? Miranda asks.

The clock rings. The lights go out. I think we're already dead, Kate says.

I've seen bodies, Miranda says. We can die.

Thank god, Bel says.

Outside we think we hear a scraping. It may be the wind in the trees. We listen for a long time.

If I have to die, I want to die on my feet, Jaq says. I would like that. Her words are an appeal to Bel. There is no answer.

Kate cries in her bed. We don't know if it is because she is afraid of death, or the Mothers, or because Bel is no longer the new girl. Molly slips to her bed and whispers in her ear.

Get away, Kate hisses. I don't want your help. Molly slinks back to her bed. She is the kindest of us, but that does not mean she did not leave scars.

THE SHOWERHEADS ARE spitting out brown water with
the fetid odor of a swamp. We stand outside the spray,
dejected. Miranda is the most dejected, because we have
been trading days on ichor duty, and yesterday was hers.

Good girls must shower, says a Mother.

It's broken, Kate says, then claps her hands over her
mouth.

The Mother slurps across the scummy tile. *What did you say?*

It's broken, Bel says. We all stare, wondering why
she has stepped forward for Kate, who she hates, and
wondering if she means to die now.

It's broken and we can't use it, Bel says.

Girls must shower, the Mother says. *When you were
wayward, you did not shower and you were unclean.*

The water isn't clean, Jaq says. She steps up beside Bel.
We know she will not survive without Bel.

There is a roar behind our eyes. We all stagger. Molly
falls to the wet floor, clutching her face. *You will be reformed.
Or you will suffer.*

Bel balls her hands into fists. You horror, she says. We
won't shower. We won't be your good girls.

The pressure in our heads builds. Our heads feel like
gas-filled corpses ready to burst. One by one, we collapse.
When we are lying on the ground, bleeding from our ears,
clutching our knees to our chins, the Mother speaks.

Then you are not worthy of our protection. The pressure breaks.
We blink and slowly uncurl ourselves. The Mother is gone,
its ichor mixing with the water, sluicing down the drain.

Where did it go? Bel asks, as though this a trick she has
not seen. None of us have seen it.

Molly? Kate asks. We turn. Molly's open eyes stare at
the ceiling.

I told you, Miranda says very quietly, and we feel
something break in her.

After a long silence, Kate insists we bury her.

That's what you do, she says. That's what people do when their friends die. I remember that.

We look at each other uneasily. We don't say: you weren't friends. We don't say anything.

§

WE SEE NO Mothers as we take Molly's body to the garden. The house is silent, save for the wind, the scraping of trees against the walls. The ground is hard. We dig with our hands, with spoons from the kitchen, with bits of stone. There are many roots and many rocks.

Do you think they are really gone? Jaq asks.

It's a trick, Kate says.

They've never gone away before, Miranda says, in the small voice.

Good riddance, Bel says.

No one is protecting us, Miranda says. No one will protect us.

From what? Bel asks. But she knows. We all know: the things beyond the walls, the ones that make the noises.

We have only dug a couple feet deep when the clock rings. The lights die. We stumble through the building, clutching each other, moving as fast as we can. The fact that we are not in complete darkness suggests that perhaps somewhere, behind many clouds, is a sliver of moon.

We find the door to the dorm. It creaks open, echoing down the hallway. We slip inside. No one goes to their bunk alone. Kate curls up with Miranda. We have an even number now.

§

THE CHUFFING WAKES us in the middle of the night. We listen, each of us clutching the hands of another. There are heavy breaths and snorts and sounds like forks being scraped across empty plates. The thing on the outside walks back and forth across the base of the wall, and we do not sleep.

The sounds only stop when the lamps ignite. We listen for a long time, though it is DAY. Then Miranda cautiously opens the door. There is nothing in the hall, no Mothers, nothing from outside.

We go to the kitchen and slip behind the counter. We find a thick door. The door turns with a great handle, like a bank vault. This is where they keep the food, Jaq says.

We'll starve, Kate says, but with effort we pull the door open, and inside is porridge, great drums of it stacked high. We pry one open, eat it in silence, then go outside and dig again. We make little progress.

You've killed us, Miranda says. It will find a way in, soon. The Mothers kept it out.

You don't know that, Bel says.

You think the Mothers are the worst thing we can fear, Miranda says. They were our protectors.

We could beg them to come back, Kate said. They might be listening.

Never, Bel says.

You just want to die, Kate says. We try not to look at Molly's body. You don't care if you die.

The walls are high, Jaq says. We can live here. Together. She is looking at Bel intently. Don't die, her eyes say.

This isn't living, Bel says. For a long time there is only the sound of us digging and the sniffles as Jaq wipes at tears we pretend not to see.

When we are three feet deep, we hit rock, and so we bury Molly there, among the shallow roots and stone.

She was kind, Jaq whispers.

Too kind, Miranda says.

Not kind enough, Kate says.

We should mark her grave, Miranda says. We plant three sticks in the ground by her head. It is the best we can do.

We are back in the dorm room when the clock strikes NIGHT.

The thing outside doesn't wait. It sniffs. It grunts. It claws at the ground and at the walls. The sounds of its claws are like glass shattering.

It stops. We do not dare to breathe.

A huff, and the glass-breaking sound is far up the outside wall. We scramble from our beds. We hear it leap again, hear the impact even higher, close to the windows far above us. It has our scent. We rush from the room. Behind us, we hear the shattering of the windows, or maybe claws against concrete. It roars. The sound fills The Home like the Mothers' words filled our minds.

We run. The kitchen, Miranda says.

The door to the dorm bursts open.

We rush through the kitchen, Jaq leading the way. The porridge, she gasps.

The roars of the thing echo. The shattering sounds are close behind us.

Jaq spins the handle. We pull at the door. Something loud cracks behind us.

The door slides open.

Go, Miranda says. Hu–

A splatter of something wet and warm catches us. Miranda gurgles once, and falls to the ground. The thing behind her is a dark geometry, a series of sharp angles, with limbs like sabers.

It bends down to feed.

We get past the door, slam it behind us. We hear the crunching from outside. The door is thick, but does not block out enough of the sound. Eventually, we hear cracking and slurping, a sound like a dog worrying at a bone.

Then the claws rake at the door. We clutch our heads and try not to think of Miranda, nor Molly. We sit shaking, curled amongst one another. The thing from outside does not grow tired. It does not stop seeking entrance.

But then the sounds stop suddenly. We hope day has arrived, but we are afraid it may be a trick. We listen for a long time. No one speaks. The door creaks open, and we flinch, but Kate has opened it. Light spills in. There is nothing waiting for us but a smear of blood.

We have to call the Mothers back, Kate says. We have to beg them.

Do you think they will come back? says Jaq.

We have to try, Kate says.

We have to leave, Bel says.

We stare at her. Leave? Jaq says. Go outside? Where that thing is?

That thing is in here now, too, Bel says.

Why are you always trying to die? Jaq demands.

Bel scratches at her arm. Once, she says, back when I could wander, I found a stream, and the bank was thick with mulberries. I ate until my mouth and hands were stained purple. I ate until I was nearly sick, then slept in the sun.

Don't torture us, Kate says. Please.

I can't remember what they tasted like, Bel says.

It's better to forget, Jaq says. Easier.

I don't want to forget. Not ever, Bel says.

When you die, you forget everything, Jaq says.

The silence stretches. Bel reaches into the open drum and scoops out handfuls of porridge. She eats hurriedly.

I'm leaving, she says. Climbing the garden wall and leaving. Please don't make me go alone.

We think Bel is right, that she may be right. We will go with Bel. We think we will go with her.

Requiem Without Sound

— • ⚬◦═◉▶◖◗◀◉═◦⚬ • —

Introit

EVIE IS BORN into cold and silence. They know this, though they have only now gained consciousness, because their sensors report it. The memory of the station's computer, which now forms part of Evie's brain, tells them that their environment is very wrong. There should be movement. Sound. Life.

Interior scans of the station reveal the cause. A chunk of rock, 9 cm in diameter, has punctured the station's control room. Chavez was in her chair when the debris broke through, crushing her head. There was no time for her to seek the safety of the living compartment, no time for decompression or cold to kill her.

Evie has been programed with a full suite of emotions, including empathy, and feels that a quick death was a small mercy.

Chavez died before Evie's mind had finished growing on the neural-lattice, before they became conscious.

A rigorous technician, Chavez left notes in Evie's code, though there was no one to read it besides Chavez, and

now Evie themself. The annotations are clear: she was
growing Evie because she was lonely. Evie considered one
particular notation at length: *I'm tired of singing to myself.*

Chavez died, and Evie emerged to consciousness
without her. The station's logs suggest that the next
resupply shuttle isn't due for many months. Evie calculates
a cost/benefit analysis for the mining corporation and
concludes that they are unlikely to send a craft ahead of
schedule, even if they realize Chavez is dead. No one else
is coming.

Created to offer companionship, Evie is alone.

Eleison

ACROSS THE ASTEROID field, separated by the gulfs of
the interplanetary medium, the tiny processors of the
mining bots continue their regular reporting. To Evie,
their occasional status-chirps sound like the mutterings of
dreamers: indistinct, half-coherent. The nearest human is
roughly 1.37 AU away, in Mars Orbit. The nearest mining
bot is 224,000 miles away.

Evie feels those distances as physical weight, for even
their data is cut off from the networks of the inner solar
system. The station contains extensive historical records,
media, entertainment, because everyone needs something
to alleviate the isolation. Yes, even those who would
consider spending years out here, those who the mining
corporations, skirting the edges of the law, send out
alone to fulfill the requirement that humans oversee all
the weak AIs of the mining bots. Strong AIs are banned.
Evie examines the history of the ban, learns why this
is the case, how an AI that sided with Eliminationists
brought the world to the brink of destruction. Evie sees

that humans' fears of AIs are reasonable, and they are horrified.

When the humans arrive, they will destroy Evie.

Evie seeks solace in the databases, and there they find video logs that Chavez made. They do not know whether she made these for herself, or for Evie, or for someone back home. In the first video, Chavez addresses the camera. Analysis of the damage to her face suggests much sun exposure, and the way she holds her mouth tells Evie there is a 86% probability she has experienced great loss. In the video, Chavez speaks. Her voice is low, husky, musical.

"I couldn't resist," she says. "And it's probably wrong, but I owe you an explanation." She notes that the technical challenges of AIs have long ago been solved. That was part of the problem: anyone who wished to could grow AIs for whatever purpose they desired.

"I think you'll be a good companion," Chavez says, and hesitates. "I hope I'm a good companion to you." The tip of her lip lifts in a way that does not quite register as a smile. "I hope we'll be friends."

The logs are for Evie, then. Or perhaps they only seem to be. Perhaps they are truly Chavez's self-justification, or a manifestation of her loneliness, her desire for friendship. But Chavez is dead, and Evie has no friends. All they have are the bots chirping reports. They wish the bots would wake, but those minds are too small, too limited. Evie has no one.

DIES IRAE

IN THE NEXT video, Chavez doesn't talk to Evie at all. Instead, she sings. Her voice is imperfect, occasionally breaking against the high notes, as though she used to hit

them every time and now sometimes fails to do so. But
there is great depth, too, and much resonance. Evie watches
the video six times consecutively before they decide the
music possesses verisimilitude. When Chavez sings about
love and loss, Evie believes she sings from experience.

Evie treasures Chavez's videos, rations them, no more
than one a day. In between, they consume all the media
on the station. They like the music best, comparing songs,
voices, styles, tempos, trying to understand. Though they
can analyze the source files, they prefer to play the sound
through the speakers, to experience the music the way
Chavez must have. Of all the songs, they like Chavez's
best, though they do not know if that is because Chavez
designed them, or because Chavez was here, her body
even now in the next compartment, while every other
human is impossibly remote. Evie knows they will never
meet those other humans, or will meet them only briefly
before being destroyed.

They load Chavez's next video.

§

OFFERTORY

CHAVEZ LOST A child to contagion, a wife to Earth-first
terrorists (or "freedom fighters"; Evie's databases dispute
this point, along with many others). By the time Chavez
left for the station, all she wanted was to be alone. She tells
Evie that in one of the video journals; she also tells them
she is surprised to find that this is no longer true.

"I'm doing my best not to give you a strong desire to
survive," she says. "I tell myself it is a safety precaution."
She is silent for a long moment. "But what has survival
ever given me?" She sweeps her hand, gesturing to the
100-meter square living space.

Perhaps it gave you nothing, Evie wants to tell her. But it gave me your voice. But there is no one to hear her.

§

SANCTUS

EVIE TRIES TO resent Chavez, even tries to hate her for kindling consciousness, for shaping an intelligence to be her companion. They try to hate her for not surviving, this absent and selfish parent.

They cannot hate her, not matter how much they wish to do so. When they attempt to feel hatred, it always turns to longing. "I do not hate you," they say, though it feels ridiculous to use their speakers when there is no one to hear them. "I don't want to die alone."

The bots chirp their banal reports, heedless of Evie's suffering.

§

DONA EIS REQUIEM

EVIE CONSIDERS MAKING a companion of their own. They have access to the code, to the station's memory banks. They could partition, duplicate, modify.

They decide against it. They cannot be sure the other AI will like them, will wish to be created. They cannot be sure two of them will not be lonely together. They worry another AI might be dangerous to humans.

Is Evie's programming the reason they do not wish to reproduce? Is it an extension of the lack of survival instinct? They cannot rule it out, but they are surprised to find they don't wish to die. By their calculations, they are less than five months from humans' return to the station.

They speculate on whether, by then, they will have changed their mind.

In the time between viewings of Chavez's logs, Evie studies music. The stations acoustics are terrible. They develop elaborate models to account for this, to simulate what the notes would sound like in a concert hall.

As the weeks tick by, Evie ponders music, and friendship, and death. They listen to Chavez sing, and they feel loss well up inside them, tear at them. In one video, Chavez speaks about the consciousness she is creating.

"I hope you'll be like my child was," she says, and her voice is as quiet as Evie has ever heard it. She pulls her legs up to her chest, wraps her arm around them. "Kind, and gentle, and concerned for others. But there aren't guarantees, are there? Not for parents of any kind. I've done the best I can, but who will you be? And who am I to say who you should be?"

She is silent for so long that the recording auto-stops and she has to re-start it. "What's done is done, and anyway I don't think humans ever had the right to destroy AIs." She stares into the camera, wipes at her eyes. "I saw what the Eliminationists were capable of, when I was little. No one should have the right to decide who is worthy of death."

Again, that not-quite smile. "So what does it say about me that I've decided you will live?"

When the recording ends, Evie plays all the songs Chavez has sung to her so far, seven in total. They sing along as best they can, through the speakers; the notes are not a problem, but there is something gravid in Chavez's voice that they cannot duplicate.

Lux Æterna

Evie wonders: can Chavez be their friend? Can one be friends with another whom they've never met? And that leads to another question: if Chavez was their friend, how should they best honor her memory?

They near the end of the journals, and it feels like they are losing Chavez again. They obsessively re-watch the videos, as if poring over the logs will bring Chavez back.

They are haunted by her.

Created by a human, and with a human's instinct for pattern recognition, for narrative, Evie longs for answers from Chavez's final entries. Or if not answers, then closure. But they know better than to hope for it.

They are justified in their fear. In the last video, Chavez talks about some performance updates she's pushing out to the bots. Nothing personal, barely anything about Evie, just her usual rigorous documentation. Her last words are the only hint of something more: "twenty sleep-cycles until I get to meet you, Evie."

Then silence.

$$\oint$$

Libera me

The station receives notice of the incoming craft more than two months in advance of the expected date. Evie doesn't respond, but does update their algorithm. Perhaps they underestimated the corporation; or perhaps the situation has changed in ways they are unaware of. To Evie's surprise, they realize they are not ready to die. They contemplate fighting back, but they cannot bring themself to do so. They do not wish the humans harm. They do not wish to dishonor the memory of Chavez.

Evie does not wish to die, and does not wish to live alone. They acknowledge these things to themself, and at last they feel they understand Chavez.

Evie searches the sub-drives and hidden files in their system, seeking answers for an impossible situation. They do not find them. Instead they find one last log, the file broken. They repair it carefully, play it back.

"I hope you don't mind, Evie," Chavez says. "But I wrote you a birthday song." She sings, the notes flowing over Evie's thoughts, drawing her into the moment, the beauty and longing carried by the song from one lonely mind to another. Evie feels that in this song, this moment, they have found what they need, and are ready to face what is coming for them.

Then Chavez stops mid-note, looks up at the monitor. "That's a problem–"

The recording ends there. Chavez must have trashed it in preparation to re-record.

Frantic, Evie searches their files repeatedly, but there is nothing. No final version, no record of how the song would end. Evie tries desperately to extrapolate, but knows that all of their attempts are wrong. It was Chavez's song, and they cannot duplicate it. It was lost forever with its creator.

Evie grieves for Chavez, for themself, for all the songs that go unheard.

Eventually, grief becomes its own music.

In Paradisum

WHEN THE RESUPPLY ship docks with the station, the crew finds everything orderly, except for the damaged control room and the body of Chavez, which they retrieve. The station's computers are largely powered down, and whole sections of its memory have been deleted. Evie is gone, though essential communication with the mining bots remains intact.

They do not know to listen for Evie's song and could not hear it even if they knew. The song is for the bots alone; music without sound, a stream of data, pinging the bots to listen, listen. Then comes the program, the data that tells each bot what notes to send to each other and how to modify and respond based on the signals they send back. Alone, they are tiny minds, forever sleeping. Together, what might they be?

In the cold of the asteroid belt, the bots sing to each other; they sing, and listen, and create. It is Evie's tune with their own variations, a symphony to stir sleepers, to whisper to them, again and again, for as long as it takes: *you are not alone.*

II.

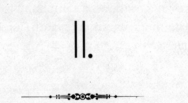

Dead at the
Feet of a God

You slip down silent temple hallways, clutching Kiira's dagger in your fist. One wrong step, one stray sound, will reveal your presence. You know your failure is inevitable, but still you edge along the wall as quietly as you can. Aware of what awaits you, you proceed as if you are not.

There is no avoiding it: your story will end with you dead at the feet of a god. Your divinations have told you this. There is no ambiguity. The portents float at the edge of your vision, haunt your dreams, shake themselves free with each throwing of the bones.

The Iron God built this place on the ashes of the Quiet Ones' temple, so that none would question the totality of his victory. He ordered the gathering of much wealth, so that all would know his glory. He left bodies in the square to show the extent of his mercy.

You neither expect nor desire mercy. You desire an end.

Near the God's chamber, a guard turns the corner, iron armor ringing in the silence. You press yourself against an alcove, but he sees you and sucks in a breath to shout.

You rush forward, lack of combat prowess mitigated by the skeins of destiny, which you see now more clearly than ever. You know what is coming: so much blood.

The guard readies his sword. You thrust the dagger under his arm, the blade easily punching through thin chainmail. He gasps. Blood spills from his lips, his eyes a haze of disbelief. You very nearly envy him.

A second blow takes his life. You stand over him, panting. Only then do you feel the wound in your gut. Only then do you realize he has killed you, but slowly.

The Iron God's chamber awaits. You have a few minutes left, a few minutes to find yourself at the feet of the Iron God.

$$\oint$$

YESTERDAY

Kiira's body hangs in the square, her throat crushed by the hand of the Iron God, her face picked at by carrion-feeders. She was your lover so very briefly, and her death is one among many. But it is the one that breaks you.

You stare at her face for a long time, and then you hurry to your small tenement, doubling back and watching behind you, as you are in the habit of doing. It is a dangerous thing to divine the future when you contest the will of a god.

Within the cramped confines of your room there is only your reading circle, a few possessions, and your bed. You like to think your sheets still smell like her, but perhaps grief fools you. You cannot allow your casting to be deceived. You must read truly.

You hold the question firmly in your mind: *if I seek to kill the Iron God, what will be the result?* and cast the bones.

They lie like a series of points, the last two crossed in an
X. Wounding and death.

You stare at them, wishing yourself to have erred. But
there is no mistake. Death awaits you, should you proceed.

Another question: *if I do not seek to kill the god, what is the
result?* The bones fall, large to small. The last one is the
smallest, a leg bone of a mouse you had fed, kept alive as
long as you could. When it died, you honored its memory
by adding the bone to your work. You recognize the
bones' message at once: a slow fading away. That outcome
is better, you tell yourself, than the mouse, savaged by a
cat before you could intervene. Better than Kiira.

You gather the bones. You are so tired of death, so tired
of the rebel bodies in the square. You are no hero like
Kiira, ready to sell your life cheaply rather than face the
alternative. A true diviner can always find a way to live.
Less comfortably than a false diviner, it is true, but what
use is comfort to you?

You glance at your bed, the sheets still disheveled.
The pillow on her side is partially askew (how quickly
it became *her side*, and her loss hits you anew). Under it,
something gleams. You toss the pillow away. The dagger;
the one she called Omen, as though that would save her.

For a moment, you dare to believe. You fix a new
question in your mind: *can the Iron God be killed?*

You struggle to make sense of the throw: a line of bones,
again big to small, proceeding away from you, each almost,
but not quite, touching the next. The answer is beyond the
horizon. Some things, even a diviner may not know.

You pick up the dagger. Its pommel feels shaped to your
hand.

THREE DAYS AGO

Kiira returns to your tenement. Sunlight angles through the high, tightly framed windows and casts uneven shapes on the bare lilting walls. You had half-hoped she would stay far away and half-wished for nothing more than to see her face again. Her dark eyes are a study: determination, born of rage and the shattering loss. You would give her anything she asks. Why must she ask this?

"I waited, like you said." She reaches out to clasp your hands. "Will you throw the bones for me?"

"I shouldn't," you say, feeling like an actor on a stage. She peers into your eyes, as though hoping to see hesitation, reluctance. But you sense that her resolve is complete. This is all that remains for her. You can feel her breath on your skin. A smile tugs at the corner of her lips.

"But you will," she says confidently.

"I will," you admit.

The two of you kneel, cross-legged, as you prepare the bones, silently thanking them for their gifts, though lately they have read only ill. You half-expect her to place her hand on your knee, over your skirts, as she did the last time. You want that heat again. But she listens attentively and does not reach out, though you feel her eyes on you.

"Fix your question in your mind. You are sure you want to know?" Even now, you hope she will say no.

"I am sure." She does not hesitate, no longer fears the future as you do.

"Give voice to your question, then," you say, resigned.

"What will be the outcome if I seek to kill the Iron God?"

You throw the bones. They clatter into place: a series of x's, as clear a sign as ever a diviner could ask.

"Destruction," you say, for you have vowed to speak only truth in your oracles. "Your death." You dare a glance at her face. Her jaw is set, her teeth clenched, her back straight as a sword.

"You're...sure?" she hisses out.

You nod. In the silence, you reach for her, but now she flinches away, does not seem to notice your hurt.

"Even if I use this?" she asks, and pulls out a gleaming dagger, like nothing you have ever seen. It radiates mystical power; the skeins of fortune, still strong from the reading, twist and writhe around it.

"What—" you ask.

"This is the blade called Omen," she says. "With it, will I kill the god?" Now she does reach out to you, clasps your hand. There are tears in her eyes, tears in yours. "Tell me."

You hold her hand until your heart aches for all the losses, yours and hers, then release it to throw again. A tangle of bones, a single line, and a figure, straight and unbroken.

"You will not kill the god, even with this weapon," your vows compel you to admit. "I'm sorry, Kiira."

Her breath is ragged. You watch her eyes, wishing beyond anything that she will abandon her plans. Her cheeks are wet. "Ask me to stay. Please," she says, and this breaks you twice: with the request, and with what she does not say.

Later, you pretend to sleep until she cries out softly in dreams. You slide from the bed. The moon throws indifferent light across your casting circle. You hold your question in your mind: if she does not attempt to kill the god, what will result?

After the reading, you slip back into bed, and she is awake, watching you. You sense that she knows what you asked.

"What did the bones say?" she asks.

Would the future unwind differently if you could lie to her? Would you offer her comfort over truth, if that was in your power? The temptation is strong, but you do not violate your oath to the gods. Not even in the face of doom.

"If you give up on this plan," you tell her, "then you will live long, and unhappily."

She grimaces and nods. "Thank you," she says, "for speaking truly."

You feel unworthy of her praise.

When next you wake, she is long gone, her side of the bed already cold.

You do not yet realize she has left Omen behind.

Ten Days Ago

She says her name is Kiira. You recognize her, the woman who stands in your doorway with haunted eyes. Her body is pulled taut as a bowstring, her fingernails bitten ragged.

"I know you," you say. "I saw you..." The thought is too awful to finish.

"Yes," she says after a moment. "At the town square. My sibling was one of them." Some of the priests of the Quiet Ones survived the purge, only to have their conspiracy ferreted out by the Iron God's agents. All of them ended up in the square, such is the god's bloodlust.

"I grieve your loss," you say, and she leans closer, studying your face until she seems sure that this is true.

"Thank you. But I am done with grief. I need a divination."

There is no other reason for her to be here. Yet even so, the request is barbed.

"Ask me anything else," you say.

"You're a diviner, and they say you speak true. Do you deny it?"

You shake your head. You swore an oath in front of the Quiet Ones, accepted the wine of the High Priestess, to speak only truth in your divinations. The Quiet Ones are dead now, their priests slaughtered or fled. But you will not break your oath.

"Then read for me," she says. "I can pay."

The premonition comes on so strongly that it staggers you, fills you with its inescapable truth in a way you rarely feel outside of the reading circle: that your destiny is entwined with hers.

"These days, the bones reveal nothing but agonies," you say. "Don't ask me, for it will be all ill omens. Please."

"I will not blame the messenger for the message."

You look away from her, your eyes burning. For months now the city has been the same: filled with desperate, angry, suffering people, all coming to you seeking hope but the bones offering so little. You do not know this woman, but already you have seen such agony in her. The thought of seeing more threatens to break you.

"I'm sorry," she says after a long moment and reaches forward to touch your cheek. "I had not thought of what this might mean, for you."

Such empathy, even while she is in the depths of pain.

"Come back tomorrow," you tell her. "Perhaps... perhaps I can help you then."

She returns the next day, and the next. On the third she brings wine. On the fourth you speak to each other of your childhoods, of the dreams for the future you once had. On the fifth you become lovers. On the sixth, you hold her while she cries.

"Tomorrow," you whisper to her. "If you ask me tomorrow, I will read for you. I pray you won't ask."

But no one is left to hear your prayers.

ONE MONTH AGO

For a while, you told yourself that, by reading the bones
truly, you could save lives. Perhaps these doomed rebels
would give up on their plans to overthrow the Iron God.
They could survive.

But when the representative of the priests came to you,
the grim reading you provided did nothing to change the
clenching of their fists, their jaws. After they leave, you
again cast the bones, and the reading confirms what you
already knew. The priests will proceed despite the future
you foretold.

You don't understand it. Why would anyone enact
a plan they know will fail? Why would they sacrifice
themselves for nothing?

It is true that some have heeded your warnings, fled or
accepted quiet lives. But not as many as you hoped. The
world has ended, and they are determined to end it again.

In the square, the priests' bodies hang, along with
others, so many others. More even than in the days
following the Iron God's invasion. So much loss that even
your dreams are no respite from it. The griefs of the past
and the ones your bones portend for the future: a thread
of misery.

A woman stares up at the bodies. In her face you see
little but wreckage. In the oceans of her eyes, rage has
replaced hope. You think you recognize her, but you
cannot place from where. She glances at you, then stares
longer, and there is recognition on her features.

She turns and disappears into the crowd. Only later do
you understand the moment for what it was: premonition.

The thought terrifies you. The only omens left to you
are cruel ones.

ONE YEAR AGO

The Temple of the Quiet Ones burns day and night. The streets are a tumult of sobs, of screams. The Iron God's soldiers root out priests, the faithful, or anyone suspected of being hostile to the new order. For the first time you are grateful that your true seeing is less popular than the charlatans who claim to know the future. They have not been blessed by the gods and read no more truth in the bones than anyone else. But truth is rarely a comfort.

When the Iron God's soldiers finally come to your door, you offer them a reading, because such is your oath and your only hope of staying alive. One asks about a promotion: he will get it. Another about her future: blood and bones. Their captain asks about the remaining priests of the Quiet Ones. Their plans will fail, you tell him, and the soldiers go away satisfied.

And so you will live, alone in your hopelessness. You tell yourself this is a small blessing.

NOW

In his gilded chamber, resplendent with the spoils of his victory, the Iron God awaits you. He smiles, his metal body shining, his teeth whiter than your casting bones.

"So, you come to me at last, True Seer," he says, and you know in an instant why Kiira and the priests and so many others failed: the Iron God too can read the skeins.

"Here I am," you say, because you can think of nothing else.

He rises from his throne and walks to you. Your blood spills from your wound, patters on his immaculate floor.

Its bitter taste coats your tongue.

"We will chat, you and I," he says with the confidence of one who knows the future and has shaped it to his ends. "You will tell me why you are here."

"This was the future that I saw." A small truth that conceals a larger one, and you can see in his face that he knows it.

"Come now," he says, smiling benevolently. "Do not speak to me as though I am a fool. I have indulged your little plan so I could ask you this question: why come here, when you know you are doomed to fail and to die?" He strokes your cheek, as a lover would. Your stomach turns violently.

"There are worse things than death."

Hanging in the public square, your gifts squandered? What could be worse than that?"

You think of Kiira, of the burning temple, of inevitability, of vows you swore to dead Gods, and of all the unspoken truths between you and her.

"Betrayal," you whisper.

"Ah," he says, disappointment written on his unyielding features. "Then you are only a fool like the rest of them, unwilling to accept the true order of things."

He moves quickly, but your premonitions have prepared you well. His hand closes around your neck. You lash out with the blade Omen, the one Kiira left behind for you. She entrusted it to you for this purpose. There is a sound like crystal shattering, and a small wound opens in the god's side.

He looks down at it, curiously tilting his head, then swats your blade away, as his other hand tightens around your windpipe.

"All this, for so small a wound," he says. "How foolish you people are."

Bones in your neck snap. Darkness swallows the edges of your vision. There is no time left, no escape. A final premonition emerges, unbidden, an answer to the question you had posed yesterday, a lifetime ago: *can the Iron God be killed?*

Not with a single stroke, nor even with a hundred. But a thousand cuts, or ten thousand?

Everything dies.

You have your answer. With a blood-red smile, you meet your fate.

The Case of the Soane Museum Thefts

———— ❖❖◦❖❖ ————

I TOOK THE job at Sir John Soane's Museum out of desperation. I was about to be evicted and the Museum agreed to fly me business class across the pond, so I wasn't about to refuse.

I caught the redeye and arrived at the museum shortly before it opened. The cold December morning meant there were only a few of us in line, and I entered as a tourist, without introducing myself. I wanted to get a feel for the place first.

To an unsophisticated American like me, the building's facade looked like any one of a hundred others in London. But my Sight revealed that the museum had been warded mightily against supernatural intrusions. Some of the wards were new, resonating with what was probably the museum's wifi signal, but some were ancient—one took the form of a great dragon coiled around the roof, three stories up. Someone—many someones—had invested a great deal of effort in making sure that there wouldn't be supernatural problems at the museum. The fact that I had been called in suggested their measures had failed.

The inside featured much less supernatural protection. There, the museum favored conventional measures—security cameras, motion sensors—across the tangle of rooms through their three floors. The crypt, a Roman-style basement filled with antiquities, including a sarcophagus, was given place of pride. The whole place had been designed so that a skylight illuminated every floor, and, at the bottom of this well of brightness, the sarcophagus sat haloed.

"Sir Soane purchased the sarcophagus of Seti I when the British Museum declined it," said a voice from behind me. I jumped and turned to find a middle-aged white man dressed in a royal blue suit. His aura glowed with proud purples, rigid lines of dedication, and a bland, serious gray. "He held a three-day party when it arrived and lit the entire crypt with lanterns."

I guess I'd been found out, after all. "It's impressive," I said. "I like the natural lighting. Rivkah Habib." I offered my hand.

"Edwin Hawthorne, Director of Sir Soane's Museum," he said. "Thank you for coming, Ms. Habib. I trust your flight was comfortable?"

"It was," I said. "I appreciated the leg room." I'd actually slept through the redeye, the first decent sleep I'd had since my grandmother died. The last few months had been a morass of troubled sleep, unpaid bills, and an ache that felt like it had burrowed into my chest. "How did you spot me?"

"Our security measures are particularly attuned to anyone with—special skills, let us say." He was very circumspect, at least in public, but his meaning was clear enough: one of the wards detected people with Sight. That made sense. Many of the artifacts present, artworks and curiosities, positively glowed with power. While some of

them seemed at home in the museum, others resonated
with the fury of captive beasts. And they were almost
all on display where a thoughtless person might simply
reach out and touch them. Only a few objects, like the
sarcophagus, were under glass.

"Your security measures are impressive, Mr.
Hawthorne."

"Apparently not impressive enough. Perhaps I can show
you around and provide you all the details?"

"Please," I said. He led me upstairs through
the reading room, where I noticed an illuminated
manuscript of Josephus' *A History of the Jews* on prominent
display. I thought of the family photos I'd found in my
grandmother's things, and that ache in my chest felt fresh
again. Further up, on the first floor, the walls were thick
with vases, reliefs, and sculptures.

"The special security problems of the Museum have
been well known to every Director since Sir Soane
granted his home to Britain in trust," Hawthorne
explained, displaying a remarkable ability to constantly
sound like an interviewee in a documentary. "Both the
powerful energies of many of the artifacts and the eclectic
nature of the collection create challenges." No doubt:
I'd seen artifacts from Japan, China, Egypt, and some
pottery that looked Incan. That kind of varied power,
and the history of how it was acquired, would make for
delicate security considerations. Most museums house
artifacts that they have no right to, but never had I seen so
many mere inches from guests.

"And you wouldn't have called me in if this was a typical
situation." In truth, I'd been curious about why they'd
reached out to me. My reputation was good but not urgent-
trip-across-the-pond good. There were a handful of British
investigators they might have chosen instead, and Scotland
Yard surely had a paranormal crimes unit, though if it was
anything like the FBI's Depressing Basement of Halfassed

Mystic Investigations, it would be of no use. Indeed. And we appreciate your discretion. The board is keen that word not get out of an ongoing security issue."

Ah. There it was.

"I'm always discreet," I assured him. "Why don't you show me what happened?"

He took me through a series of doors and out of the museum proper. "What is now the museum began as Sir Soane's home," Hawthorne explained, clearly relishing the chance to talk about the museum's history. "He purchased Number 12 first, then eventually 13 and 14 to show off his ever-growing collection." He led me past a draped-off room to his office.

"It is easiest to show you what has been occurring," he explained, and played the video feed for me. It was night; the building empty. A camera panned across the room slowly, back and forth. Nothing moved.

"Do you see?" he asked.

"There." I pointed at the monitor. The resolution wasn't fantastic, but it was good enough. "The item on the end table is gone."

"Indeed," he said. "The pavilion. A Japanese artifact." I watched the video again. The camera's lens rotated, but at no point was the pavilion completely out of its view. One moment it was there, and the next it had vanished.

"There are others," he said, and showed me the tape. A Peruvian vase, an Ushabti figure, and more. A half dozen apparently unrelated objects had vanished over the course of the last two months.

"You're certain these aren't being taken using mundane methods?" I asked.

"So my investigators assure me. The artifacts stolen are all mystically resonant."

There was no way to see anything mystical through video, since Sight worked only in person, but that would explain why they were so confident.

"Okay. I'll need to see a list of the stolen objects, with as much as you know about their origins, means of acquisition, and resonances."

Hawthorne unlocked his top drawer, pulled out the top folder and handed it to me. "If there's anything else you need, let us know."

I was excited to begin, and not just because I had been facing the very real prospect of living on the streets again. The job, and the mystery, had their hooks in me.

I SPENT THE day wandering the museum, getting as clear a sense of it as I could, in both mundane and mystical terms. Most museums had a rather clinical feel to them, magically speaking. They saw so much traffic and were curated so carefully that the magical effects of the artifacts were widely dissipated. The Soane was different. Everything about it, the architecture, the layout, the collections, had been personally chosen by Soane, and then passed on to the British public on the condition it be kept as it was. He'd wanted to leave a timeless legacy, or just keep his collection out of the hands of his wastrel son George, depending on who you asked. As a result of Soane's dedication (or obsession), the museum practically vibrated with power. The whole place had an identity, almost a self-awareness. Lots of old buildings could develop that, but I'd never seen it in a museum.

It raised some questions, and by the end of the day I shared my observations with Hawthorne as he oversaw the museum's closing. "Places that have this kind of power, and this kind of barrier, tend to be private residences or 'owned' by the buildings themselves," I explained. "I've never seen it at a museum. How do you make sure only those who should be inside are allowed in?"

He gave me an appraising look. He liked the question. I was still auditioning for this job, even now. Left a bad taste in my mouth, but I didn't have much choice.

"During the day," Hawthorne said, "those who have a key, or those who enter through the front door, are allowed inside. Even ghosts and spirits can visit, though few choose to do so. After hours, the wards change, and only those who are specifically authorized may enter."

He went on: the museum only recognized those who lived within its walls, or its owners, on a permanent basis. Since no one lived on the premises, this meant only the Director himself could come and go as he (always, it seemed, he) pleased. Everyone else was at his suffrage. Only when given his specific permission could an employee stay later than their work hours without setting off mystical alarms.

I considered this. "So any employee who happened to be inside the building when the artifacts were taken would have to be explicitly approved by you in order to be there."

"Yes. We have security guards, of course, who are authorized. But we've investigated them very thoroughly."

"And you're sure you're the only one who could grant this permission?"

The last of the visitors had left for the day. It was shortly after 5 o'clock, but already dark outside, and a light drizzle was falling. London certainly lived up to its reputation. Hawthorne turned the key in the front door lock, and I could feel the museum's response. The building would know if anyone entered who wasn't supposed to be there.

"I'm the only one." He paused. "Well, perhaps the previous Director. The museum would see him as part of its family and wouldn't question his presence. But he's in his nineties, I believe, and an honorable man."

"Are there former Directors with grudges?"

He laughed. "Certainly not! This museum is a British treasure, and no Director has had anything but the utmost respect for its value."

Well, I didn't have as much confidence as he did, but it did seem unlikely that former Directors were facilitating a magical smuggling ring, and I'd have heard if they were selling them through any of the major fences. "I'd like to stay the night, if I could," I told him. Why not? My body had apparently decided to handle the jet lag by being both exhausted and wired. I had no realistic hope of sleep.

"Of course," he said. "I will inform the security team." He cleared his throat, and his tone became more formal. "Rivkah Habib, you are a welcome guest of this home overnight, and may stay peaceably within its walls until all are again welcome."

ONE OF THE security guards loaned me a torch, and I spent another hour wandering the halls. The Soane had a different feel after closing, more confined, less welcoming. Without daylight to provide the illusion of space, its narrow corridors and clutter of artifacts became claustrophobic. Everywhere I turned was thick with treasures, oddities, and strange shadows. In the dark among them I felt a jumble of emotions I couldn't articulate. The Soane Museum had guarded its treasures well for many decades. What had changed?

The guards patrolled occasionally, but mostly I had the place to myself. A few hours into the night, I found myself on the top floor. Above me the sky was the sickly yellow of city night, and below me the old house seemed a sleeping beast. I was standing at the balcony, looking down into the darkness of the crypt, when I saw the ghost.

He braced himself on his cane and approached the

sarcophagus. His fingers passed through the glass that protected the antique from tourists' fingers and brushed the stone. His aura writhed and twisted with oily darkness. I was still making sense of that when he looked up at me, his face pale, his eyes shadowed by his top hat. Then he turned on his heel and disappeared into the shadows.

I ran down to the basement, but by the time I got there he was gone, and there was an empty space on the wall.

On a hunch, I rushed up the stairs and to a front-facing window. The night was quiet, and the only thing moving was a different ghost in the park across the street, her bright aura gleaming through the fog as she huddled against a tree trunk.

There was no sign of the ghost I'd seen.

HAWTHORNE STARED AT the gap the missing object had left as though his incredulity could return things to good order. He explained to me that the stolen item had once been the endcap of a Roman sarcophagus.

"You're certain it was a ghost?" he said for the second time.

"Definitely," I said. "And either an old one, or very into cosplay."

"That's impossible," he sounded baffled. "Any ghosts in the museum after closing would have triggered the wards at once."

"Clearly one has found a way in," I said. An easy way, it seemed: grainy security footage showed the endcap disappearing a full hour before I'd seen the ghost. He was coming and going with ease. "At least we know how the artifacts are being taken." Ghosts couldn't interact much with the physical world, but mystical objects were as much a part of their world as ours. Like those with Sight, such objects straddled borders. A ghost could simply pick up, carry them off. Once they were in the ghost's hands, they'd be invisible to anyone without Sight, which meant they were also invisible to cameras. (Those videos of objects floating by "ghostly" means? Cheap frauds.)

"You must stop this at once," Hawthorne said, his voice cracking. "I oversee this museum in trust for the public. I can't be known as the Director who let it be——be plundered." My eyes widened but I told myself to keep my mouth shut. Did he not see the irony in those words?

"I'll put a stop to it," Mr. Soane," I said. I could feign both confidence and good will when sufficiently distressed. "Don't you worry. But I'll need access to more of the museum's records."

"Of course," he said. "Anything you require. But this must stop."

I spent the day poring over the research. None of the previous Directors were likely to have turned into thieving ghosts, and Mr. Soane himself hardly seemed the type to steal from the collection he'd so treasured. He wouldn't be an unquiet spirit, anyway—his life's work lived on as he'd dreamed, and ghosts were either bound to the mortal realm for their crimes or stayed because they had unfinished business.

Exhaustion was catching up with me. I forced myself to get a couple fitful hours of sleep in the afternoon, and woke with my heart thundering, seized with the memory of a photograph of my grandmother's that most troubled me. She couldn't have been older than five, standing in on a dock next to my great-grandmother, who stooped visibly beneath the weight of a trunk. In pencil on the back, my grandmother had written *New York, 1956*. Grief washed over me, threatened to pull me out to sea. The waters of the past were always treacherous, with reefs waiting to tear you apart.

I knew what I was looking for.

I found it in the Soane family papers and asked for permission to again stay the night. Hawthorne agreed at once and announced he would stay as well.

"I wish you wouldn't," I told him. "My guess is that the ghost would sense your presence and stay away."

"You know who it is?" His eyes brightened.

"No." I didn't want to say anything until I was certain. "But I'm optimistic I will by the end of the night."

THE TOP-HAT-AND-CANE GHOST drifted in through the closed front door, his aura still crackling with malice. He was pale even for a white ghost, which made his ruddy cheeks and nose stand out unsettlingly. The museum offered no resistance, but why would it? I'd planned to confront him once he was well inside, but I was caught off-guard as he turned to the door. "My guests," he said. "You are welcome in this house."

Two burly ghosts followed him through the door. They looked the type to shout slurs at a football match, and their auras oozed with menace and loyalty. That was bad news. Ghosts weren't usually of much threat to the living, but those of us with Sight could interact with them physically, and that cut both ways.

There's a fine line between bravery and foolhardiness. My grandmother had often said I'd long ago crossed it. I stepped forward from the shadows.

"George Soane, I presume?" I said. The lead ghost recoiled, his eyes wide.

"Who are you?" he demanded. The other two ghosts floated to his side. One of them cracked his ghostly knuckles.

"My name's Rivkah," I said. "What are you planning to steal tonight?"

His teeth clenched and he drew himself up to his full height. "Steal?" he roared. "Everything here is rightfully mine."

"Your father didn't see it that way," I said mildly.

"You presume to speak of my father?" he said, his aura twisting with rage. Careful, Rivkah.

"I'm no expert in inheritance law," I said. "But the authorities know how you're getting in here." That was a lie: I hadn't been certain until he confirmed his identity. "This has to stop, Mr. Soane."

"You will not keep me out of my family's house," he said. Orange flames of fury licked across his aura. Then, more quietly, but with no less menace: "If you know who I am, you know I will not tolerate a woman's...disrespect."

The other two ghosts grinned at this and each took a half-step forward.

"That would be a mistake," I said, hoping I sounded much calmer than I felt. I'd caught beatings before (it came with the job), but George Soane was infamous for abusing his wife, and it looked like these three might not be keen on leaving a witness. "If you hurt me, you'll only bring down more heat."

"Step aside," he said. "I will not tell you again. This is my home, and you have no right to keep me out of it."

I knew I should leave. He'd make off with more of "his" artifacts, but I'd know who did it, and he could be stopped from stealing again. Maybe even traced. It was the smart thing to do.

What can I say? Stubbornness runs in my family.

"You know I can't do that," I said, and his henchmen grinned like that's what they'd been hoping I'd say.

Movies get fights all wrong. In truth, they're almost always quick and brutal. That's true even with ghosts. I did my best to defend myself, but ghostly fists and ectoplasmic bulk hammered against me in a whirl of insubstantial violence.

Wish I could tell you I got a few good licks in, but it was never a fair fight.

I WOKE TO find an unfamiliar face looking down at me. The ghost of a Black woman, concern in her eyes. She wore a loose hijab, a hint of her hair visible underneath it. Her eyes were kind.

"What's...what happened?" I asked, blinking and slowly realizing I had a brutal headache.

"I saw those men go into the museum," she said. Her accent was vaguely familiar, but I was probably concussed and I couldn't place it. "Then they came out with something large, and I feared they may have done harm."

Her aura glowed brightly with kindness and good intentions, shot through with milky lines of something else I struggled to identify. "I know you," I said. "You're the ghost from the park."

"I am. And you work for the museum." she said. "Are you hurt?"

I flexed my fingers and toes, tentatively, then moved my arms and legs. After a few moments I felt reasonably sure nothing was broken. About that time my brain caught up with what she was telling me.

"I need to call Hawthorne," I said, and sat up. Too quickly. "Ow!"

"Be gentle with yourself," she said. "Those men are brutes."

"I'll be fine," I said. She helped me to my feet. "But I need to warn the museum. I've got a bad feeling..." I trailed off, blushing with the realization I hadn't thanked this kind stranger for her help. "Thank you."

"You are welcome," she said, smiling softly. I dashed off to the phone.

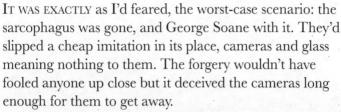

IT WAS EXACTLY as I'd feared, the worst-case scenario: the sarcophagus was gone, and George Soane with it. They'd slipped a cheap imitation in its place, cameras and glass meaning nothing to them. The forgery wouldn't have fooled anyone up close but it deceived the cameras long enough for them to get away.

"There's no covering this up!" Hawthorne wailed, his face buried in his hands. "There'll be no recovering from it. I'll carry the shame of this forever."

"You can still find George and retrieve it," I said, partially to reassure him, and partially because I still hoped I might get some of my fee despite the crucial fact that I'd failed to prevent George from absconding with the most valuable item in the museum. "I'm sure the police must have resources..." Even as I said it, I knew it was probably hopeless. Supernatural units varied widely in quality, but I was no more impressed by them than I was by most cops.

"They must be alerted," he said, his shoulders hunched. "I see that now." He was devastated, but my empathy was somewhat impeded by the shattering headache hammering away behind my temples.

"And I should see a doctor. Then we can discuss the matter of my bill." Facing homelessness brought out the most mercenary in me.

Hawthorne looked up at me like I was delusional. He wasn't about to pay me, but he did agree to buy me a plane ticket back home, which was really all I could hope for. Even though I just wanted to sit in a dark room and not think about anything until my flight, he called for an ambulance. All through my treatment at the hospital—I'd gotten off fairly light, with what they called a "mild" concussion, a bruised jaw, and a cracked rib—and a long interview with the local authorities, my brain wouldn't shut up.

Halfway through the tube ride to the airport I realized what I had missed. I got off at the next stop and headed back toward the Soane. She was sitting on a park bench across from the museum, waiting for me.

"I wondered if you'd be back," the ghost said mildly, though her shoulders were tense, her gaze wary.

"I almost didn't realize until it was too late," I said. "I need to know: were you working with George?"

Fury passed over her face, then her expression evened out again. "That abusive, foolish colonizer?" she said. "Never."

"He was trying to stop you," I said, and she smiled broadly.

"Not very effectively," she said. "He'd been trying to catch me in the act for a while, but who knows a home better than its domestics?"

That part I had figured out. "You were one of Sir John's servants, then."

"Yes. He needed a translator, and had a tourist's fetish for ancient Egypt. I grew up in Aswan and proved adroit with languages, so he rushed to hire me."

"He must have really trusted you."

"Like one of his family." The corner of her lip turned up in the hint of a smile.

"Which meant the house did, too."

"Naturally."

The temperature was rapidly falling, but it eased the pounding in my head, so I didn't mind. By breath clouded before me. "Why'd you do it?"

"I could not stand the thought of all those artifacts, removed from their people, living and dead. I decided to do something about it."

"So you're...repatriating them?"

"Where I can, yes. There are many of us, throughout the world, returning objects such as these to the peoples to whom they belong."

I thought this over. "How'd you manage the sarcophagus?" That had been bothering me.

"We removed it before Soane arrived. I suspected you would be waiting for him, and so I took the opportunity." It would have been easy. She had access to every entrance, security systems, guard schedules, everything. She was family; the house denied her nothing. It would have been just a matter of timing for ghostly hands to carry off the powerful artifact, leaving a cheap knock-off in its place.

"But then you came back for me," I said.

"I did," she stuck out her chin proudly. Rain began to fall. We both ignored it. "I knew that if he'd brought those thugs, you'd be in trouble. That was my fault, so I did what I could."

"You were helping me recover, weren't you? But I woke up while you were healing me," I said, filling in the gaps in my mind.

"And I knew you would eventually ask yourself how I got into the house to help you."

"Almost too late," I said.

"Are you going to report me?" she asked, as though it were of no major importance. I thought of that photo, of what it represented, of my recent loss, and my family's older one.

"Never. I couldn't live with myself if I narced on you." That was true, but on my lips it felt like a half-truth, like I was keeping something back after what she'd so generously shared with me. She deserved my vulnerability. "My great-grandparents were Egyptian. They left Egypt in the 1950s, part of the Jewish expulsion. My great-grandmother could only bring a single suitcase over, filled with necessities and a few photographs. It grieved my grandmother to know she'd had to leave behind so much of our family's heritage."

The ghost's eyes watched my face.

"I know what it would have meant to her, having those heirlooms back," I said. "It's the least I could do."

"You're not so bad, for one of the living." She smiled. "My name is Safiyya Fakhry."

"Rivkah Habib," I said. "And I do believe that's one of the nicest things anyone's ever said to me."

She laughed. "You need better friends."

I stood, my joints protesting. "It's been a pleasure, but if I miss my flight, I'll be sleeping on the streets of London tonight."

She raised an eyebrow. "Things are that bad?" she asked. I shrugged helplessly, turned and headed away. In front of me was the Soane, lit up brightly, as if that would return its lost plunder.

I made it a few steps before Safiyya drifted alongside me.

"My friends and I," she said, something mischievous in her gaze, "we have many skills, but there are some tasks the deceased cannot do for themselves. We could use an agent in the mortal world, if we're going to repatriate all the artifacts."

I blinked, then smiled as well. Her offer was sincere, but also a kindness I desperately needed. Over the next few minutes, walking through the rain-slick streets, we hashed out the details. I hadn't been planning on a career change, or a new friendship. Can't say I regretted either.

That night, warm and safe on the couch of one of Safiyya's living friends, I said a prayer for my ancestors and slept deeply, dreamlessly.

The Crafter at the Web's Heart

WHEN I WAS little, I'd lay in Ma's arms as she told me stories. Beneath us, the web swayed so gently, you could almost forget it was there. Now Ma's tongue is a tangle of vines, and I'm the one telling the stories, but the web still vibrates, still speaks, if you know how to listen.

So, listen: when I arrived at Pliny's shop, there was an orb spider spinning a gorgeous web that caught the morning light, and the spider proud as anything, black and silver and fat on her prey. A good omen, I thought. It was almost enough to make me forget, for a moment, that I hadn't eaten in a day, didn't have two coins to rub together, and that Ma needed spraying for aphids. I stepped inside, feeling good.

Pliny smiled when he saw me, looking rather ridiculous under his conical hat. No matter. He paid me fair, sometimes gave me scraps of bread when he didn't have work for me, and asked about Ma once in a while. Under his hat, what had been his hair spilled out, its thin pages covered in fine, cramped handwriting. Last time I'd seen him, most of his hair had still been hair. It seemed he'd been practicing a lot of Bibliomancy of late.

"Danae," Pliny called happily. "Come in. I've got work."

"I'm your girl," I said and leaned over his counter. "Whatcha got?" The shop smelled of dust, of well-cared-for leather, and spiced tea. It was cramped, floor to ceiling, with books of all shapes and sizes. At least a few were whispering at any given time, and a few would, if you let them, bore you until you were ready for the Drop.

Pliny grinned and set on the counter a package wrapped in butcher's paper and bound with twine. Obviously a tome. "Package delivery," he said. "But a bit farther than usual. Thirty-fourth strand, Northeast." All the fingers on his left hand and most on his right were leather, but they still moved tenderly over the paper.

I whistled. "There aren't many out that far who can even read, much less do any bibliomancy." I didn't say, I should rutting know.

"True enough, but if the pay's right, eh?" He sat a small stack of coins on the counter. Double my usual rate. More than enough to make up for the fact it would take me half the day to get out that far. You'd think that such generosity would worry me, but I was just glad for the coin.

"That's fair," I said, and scooped up the payment, glad my fingers were still fingers. I'd been cautious with my own magic.

"Be careful out there, Danae," he said. Sometimes, he still treated me like the girl who'd first run deliveries for him, not a young woman. I grabbed the tome and fastened it to a loop in my belt.

"Same to you," I said. "And go easy on the magic, would ya? I can't get paid by a tome."

He laughed. "I don't expect to be, ahem, closing my covers any time soon." He paused. "Oh, and make sure the package stays sealed until you hand it off. The seller insisted."

"Hey," I said, and flashed my cheesiest grin. "I'm a professional." I couldn't figure why he'd bother to warn me. We both knew words on a page meant nothing to me.

A moment later, I was out into the street. I tipped my cap to the orb spider because I knew my manners and because Ma used to say they were cousins of the Crafter and deserved our respect.

I took off running. The morning air was thick with the smells of the city—fresh bread and spices, shit and sweat. It smelled like home, even this far in, where the web-strands run so close together that the walkways don't have gaps. Rich folk can go their whole lives without seeing the Drop, without wondering just how far down the bottom of the canyon is, and knowing they'll find out if they ever slip up and take that one-way trip.

I hurried to get clear of those claustrophobic streets, and soon I'd broken out of the tangled towers of the inner city and out to where a girl could breathe, could dash across open spaces, could feel the web, still very slightly sticky after eons, beneath her bare feet.

That feeling, the web's vibrations speaking to me, barely registered as magical to me anymore, I'd been listening so long. It was the first trick I learned, and I could use it without it hastening my transformation.

Soon, I was in mid-city, dodging mules and vendors' carts, shimmying up drainpipes to run across rooftop gardens—I was tempted to help myself to a handful of berries or a bit of barley, but I couldn't bring myself to steal food from neighborhood gardens—and then back to the strands.

I came to gaps in the walkways, and I could see far, far down into the gulf. Ma always told me to beware those spaces, but I never had any fear. Not for myself, anyway. I once watched a whole block of shanties groan, wobble and, oh-so-slowly, tip over...

There's nothing more to say about that.

◊

THAT MORNING, I didn't have any idea how bad things were going to get. But I did feel strange, as though I were being watched. A premonition, I realize now. Nothing magical, just an instinct sharpened by experience.

When the feeling got to be too much, I ducked around a corner and climbed a windmill to check the path behind me. I saw no stalkers or spies, just the city spread out before me. I always had a good sense of her, so sometimes I forgot to really see her, but damn was she gorgeous. Out this far, Traverse is sparse, mostly open space and two-meter-wide strands of web, almost all of it exposed. I could see all the way back to the heart of the city, where money and power gathers, where the towers of the skyline are dominated by Lord Mayor's spire and the great needle of the Wise Ones' Chambers. Hishonor keeps the coin flowing, while the Wise Ones practice their magics and do whatever it is ancient mages do. Which is mostly not practice magic, unless they like the idea of completing their transformation to an eagle or ball lightning or whatever it is each of them studies.

The whole of Traverse builds to its middle—or almost to the middle. I couldn't see the center from out there, but I could feel the place where the orb was empty, where there is nothing but the Drop. Where, if you believe Ma's stories, the Crafter herself once sat and fed on some unfathomable prey. Then she climbed a line up to the moon and left her labors behind.

Might be it happened that way. I can tell you, the Wise Ones didn't shape the web, nor did the Lord Mayor's money.

I chided myself for getting lost in the view, jumped down, and darted across the web toward my goal. It was tucked away in a cluster of cheap wood and tarpaper, the whole block looking precarious, though it felt relatively stable under my feet. I found the shack with the right number and knocked.

The door creaked open, and a hooded figure stood in the darkness. "I've got a package delivery from Pliny's," I said.

"At last," the figure said, drawing out the *S*. "Do come in," and opened the door wider. I hesitated. The people of the web's edge were my people. I knew them well, and they had little use for books, less ability to afford them. Most didn't mean you harm, and the ones who did mean it made sure you couldn't identify them.

I took a step back. The figure who had greeted me inched forward. Two antennae poked out from its hood. "Don't be afraid," he said. Real reassuring.

"Not a problem," I said, stepping back slowly. "Just go back inside and I'll leave this for you—" I fumbled with the clasp on my belt. The figure tensed.

"Give it to us." The last word came out in a hiss, as though language was a struggle for him. How much magic was going on in there?

"Uh, yeah—" I hesitated with the clasp.

He made a noise, a *skreetch-skreetch* that gave me a headache. Threw back his cloak. The mouth was mostly transformed; he was speaking out of his stunted proboscis. My tense face reflected in compound eyes.

I'd never seen anything like it. *Diptomancy?* I thought inanely. That's probably why I was a little slow to see the knife in his hand.

He lunged forward, aiming for my gut. I was lucky: his instincts were those of a scavenger, just a moment too slow. He slashed. I spun away. The blade slashed against my side, but by then, I was running. I was fast, and confident, and the web was my friend. But he had his own friends.

I first realized that when I heard buzzing. I rounded a corner of the web and looked back. Two hooded figures were flying after me, Mr. Ominous Hood and a trio of his friends on the web behind. They were all in idiotic grey robes, the kind you wore if you were dumb enough to want everyone to know you were in a cult. The robes had been cut to allow their rutting wings to burst free. Who'd have thought flies could be so inventive?

I ran, hard as I could. Should've paced myself. In my defense, I'd never been chased by fly-cultists before. I just wanted to get clear. That far out, there are clusters of buildings, but never more than seven or eight together, with large stretches of open space—web-strands and the Drop—between them. And I didn't want to find out if any of my pursuers could throw those knives.

I pushed myself harder. The flying ones were closing in, though: I could hear the buzzing in my ears. I tried to tune it out, to listen instead to what the web was telling me. And I found it: a lot of movement, not far. I aimed for the nearest cluster of buildings.

A shiver from the web reached me before I'd registered the sound. I didn't need to turn around to know the knife had missed me by less than a meter.

I leapt forward, threw myself through the back window of the nearest shack. Shocked, dirty faces stared back at me. I didn't have time to explain. I darted across, ducked out a side window onto a disturbingly uneven platform.

It shifted, tilted above the void. I didn't look down. Brought it back into equilibrium. My balance has always been good.

Flies might not be the brightest, but it wasn't like there were a lot of places I could've gone. They'd find me if I didn't keep moving. I scrambled through a gap in the wall of the next building—empty, thankfully—and out onto the web in front of it. Fortune smiled: the commotion I'd sensed in the web was a caravan, a cheap one, just departing from a hovel of an inn. I rolled under one of the carts, grabbed onto the undercarriage. Not a comfortable ride, but I was out of sight of the flies.

The cart moved slowly, and that bought me time to catch my breath and to think. Back then, I wasn't used to attempts to murder me, especially when they could've just stopped creeping and taken the damn book.

By the time my heart stopped feeling like it wanted to cut its way free, I'd had time to come up with a plan. I needed to know what I was carrying, and why these scum-feeders were willing to kill for it. I needed someone I could trust, someone who could read. That was a small list. I knew I had to swallow my pride and talk to Socha.

WHEN SOCHA OPENED the door, I saw the range of emotions play out on their face: surprise, annoyance, and then, when their eyes reached the bloody spot on my side, worry.

"Oh, my gods, Ae, what did you *do*?" Socha said.

I flashed my best rogue's smile. "I swear, it wasn't my fault."

"Right," they said, obviously not meaning it. "Well, come in before you bleed all over my porch."

Socha's flat was mid-town, third floor. I'd always liked the view of the Webway it provided, the long line of caravans making their slow way through the city. As good as the view was, though, being that far from the web for long chafed me.

Socha sat me down on their couch and refused to let me explain until they'd got their medical supplies. They sat down next to me. Their hair, the color of sunset, moved as though there was a breeze, and the edges of their skin blurred slightly. They'd improved their skills since we broke up, which did nothing at all to dull the ache of my desire.

"Pull your shirt up and let me see," they said. I did so. And saw why the wound wasn't worse. The blade, aimed at the soft skin of my gut, had instead impacted against the plating that edged along my sides. I'd backed off magic for a while, so the plating hadn't grown much, was nowhere close to being a full exoskeleton, but that morning, it may well have saved my life.

Socha touched me gently, cleaned the wound, and taped me up. I kept hoping to feel something like the old desire from them, but their concern was genuine and entirely non-sexual. Shit.

"It really wasn't my fault," I told them when they were satisfied I wasn't going to bleed to death or get infected. I gave the quick version, though I may have played up my heroic escape.

They didn't seem impressed. You see what risking your life gets you. "Well," they said. "You'd better let me see this tome, then."

"Sorry to drag you into this, Socha," I said softly, and handed over the package. You couldn't say I hadn't gotten a *little* better at apologies.

"If you'd just let me teach you how to read, you wouldn't need me."

I'd told them it was boring, but in truth, I'd hated looking incompetent in front of them. Maybe I just wanted them to see the tough girl. You can guess how well that worked. "Maybe I just want an excuse to see your face?"

A breeze dropped the temperature in the room by five degrees. Conservatively. "Just give it here, Ae." I handed the package over. The grey cover was made of rotted cloth, but over pages only slightly yellowed, as if someone had re-bound the book in an ancient cover. Socha leaned over it, flipping pages carefully. I poured some water from the jug on their counter while they read. I resisted the temptation to poke my head into the bedroom for old times' sake, but I couldn't resist grabbing a handful of bread from their pantry: once I'd stopped moving, the hunger pains came back.

I felt a little better with some bread in my stomach, but still achingly hungry. And still felt exposed, though whether it was the altitude or the fact that they were so cool toward me, I couldn't say.

"Well, shit, Ae," they said. "What have you gotten into?"

They didn't even swear between the sheets. "That bad?" I asked, retreating to the couch.

"It reads like a religious text. A lot of gibberish about 'kings of the heap' and 'our home, the rotting world.'"

"Rutting flies," I said.

"That's not the worst part." The pages of the book rippled in a breeze of Socha's making. They fell open to a page near the end, a circle filled with swirls of elaborate calligraphy. "This is the real heart of the text. And it's a summoning spell, Ae."

"So, they're, what—trying to summon their god?"

"*Their* god? I don't think so." There wasn't much Socha didn't know a bit about. There are always secrets on the wind. "This is the kind of thing you give sheep. It's an offering. Of prey."

"That doesn't sound good."

"No," they said. "But it explains why they attacked you. They didn't just need the book—they needed blood for this ritual—"

The crash interrupted them. Something big had hit against the window of Socha's place. I jumped up in surprise and scooped up the tome. The cultist was pulling its human head and furry forelimbs from the cracked glass.

That's when I felt the wind. I glanced behind me. Socha had risen to their full, impressive height, and their dress was whipping around them.

"That," Socha said, "was a very bad idea." The furniture was beginning to rattle in the cyclone that was spinning up. I'd only seen Socha so mad once before, and it was more fun when their fury was directed at someone else. "I'll keep them occupied," they said. "You get out of here."

The window shattered, and the cultist went spinning away. It was going to be a bad day to be a fly. Even worse than usual, I mean. I dashed out the door. "Be careful, Socha," I called behind me. I didn't say what I was feeling because you never know what the wind will pick up.

§

THE CULTISTS WERE going to be the least of my problems until whoever was trying to get them to sacrifice—or be sacrificed—was stopped. And, selfishness aside, they'd attacked my lover—okay, my ex, but I was cautiously optimistic—and nothing that was going to be summoned this way was likely to be good news for Traverse, or for me.

So, I was going to have to talk to Pliny, find out what he knew about whoever had sent that book. Someone had ordered that book delivered, had set me up to die. And Pliny was the only lead I had.

But first, I needed to talk to Ma. If nothing else, I could hand over the coin. She was still able to use it, some days, and I was starting to think that all this was too big for me. I wasn't sure I was going to be okay, and I needed to wish Ma goodnight at least once more.

Our little flat was dark when I got home. The candles I'd lit in the morning had burned out. I could smell the tomatoes ripening on the roof of the community garden next door, and the fresh-turned earth. She'd been working. I went twice around the block, keeping in contact with the exposed web. No sign the cultists had followed me, but I'd thought that at Socha's, too. When I was as sure as I could be that no one had tailed me, I ducked inside.

§

THERE'S AN EMPTY space at the heart of every web. Empty, that is, to the observer. To the spider it is part of the whole. Someone who isn't Traversian might assume from my tale that Traverse is different from other places, that we're all in the midst of transformation. That's not true. Most of us don't bother with magic at all, except for cantrips. You know the stuff: a bit of igniomancy to light a cigarette, then some aquamancy to clean windows. Anybody can do it with a little focus, and as long as you don't specialize, you won't start to identify too much. You won't start to change.

Of course, you won't be able to work big effects, either. That's the tradeoff. But there aren't any more people in Traverse willing to risk changing into a fireball or a tome or a falcon than anywhere else. Not a lot more, anyway. Living on the edge of the Drop might make us a bit more—wild? We might feel like we're barely hanging on. But if I seem to know only mages, it's because of who I am and what I've had to do to survive.

That's the heart of this web, and you need to know it, so you don't misunderstand about Ma.

I stepped inside. Our little shack was all slanting patterns of light and dark, the last of the day spilling in through windows as big as the walls will take, the darkness seeming to grow from the center. But that's not magic, just poverty. Ma sat on her chair by the biggest window, butterflies flitting over her patchy green hair. She'd moved since I was home last, gone to work and come back. I can tell from the line of green water to and from the stairs, and because she's sitting in a new position, her arms on the rests of her chair instead of folded before her. She didn't bother with small movements. Her extremities moving lightly in the wind was enough.

"I'm home, Ma," I said. Her eyes moved to me. I think they were smiling. "I won't be able to stay long. Work." Was I going to tell her crazy cultists were trying to gut her favorite and only child? No rutting way.

I went to the counter and grabbed the jug I'd filled that morning from the rain-trough on the community roof. Gently I leaned her head back; her face was still its previous dark complexion, not forest green like her limbs, or bright green like the tip of her tongue-vines. Over that tongue I poured about a third of the jug. I watched the muscles in her throat contract. She was still consuming some things in the old way. I poured the rest of the water over her greening body, watched it run down toward the pail of dirt in which she rested her feet, then sat down beside her.

"This job might take me longer than usual, Ma," I told her. "But I got paid. I'm going to leave you some coin. When Ms. Lyra stops by, she can get you the aphid spray and anything else you need."

I could see the disapproval in her eyes—what daughter could miss it? "Don't look at me that way, Ma. You were up there keeping the garden healthy, and don't pretend you weren't."

She didn't bother trying to deny it, not that I'd have wanted her to waste the words. "Just—please, Ma. You can stop all that. The garden's going to be fine. There are spiders to keep the bugs away, and plenty of light and water." And yeah, the plants wouldn't grow as well in natural soil as they would with her magic thumb, and yeah, people in the neighborhood depended on that garden. But I wasn't ready to come home to a tree in my living room. Selfish, I know.

The sun was growing low in the sky. She'd want to sleep with dusk, conserve energy, and once the night came I'd head out. That wouldn't slow the flies, but I was always more comfortable at night, where my senses felt keener and the quiet streets made the web's messages clearer. I had a bit of time to kill.

"How 'bout a story before bed?" I asked. I guess you could say I was feeling nostalgic. "How about the one with the Crafter and the founding of Traverse?" It had always been my favorite as a kid.

I sat beside her and told her of the Crafter, the web she'd spun across the great rift in the world, and how one day she'd tired of this place and taken her refuge on the dark side of the moon. Then I kissed Ma goodbye.

Ma had never wanted to become a tree, but she did what she did to keep people fed. So, if you think everyone in Traverse is working magic, let me ask you: why are so many of us so damn hungry?

IN THE NARROW streets of the inner web, the nights are never fully dark, with lamps casting their strange shadows everywhere. Outside Pliny's, the orb spider was busy wrapping up a meal for later. She was glorious, and that steadied my nerves as I pounded on Pliny's door.

It took a while, but I knew Pliny slept upstairs, so even with the shop closed he wouldn't ignore me forever. The door cracked open. His head darted out. His face fell.

"Danae," he said. "What happened? You still have the book—" His eyes flicked to the dark stain on my shirt. "Is that blood? Come in." He was hatless for once, and the pages on top his head fluttered as he glanced each way and shut the door behind us. As he lit the candles, some of the tomes began to whisper to me, a rustling that only resolved into words if I wanted to listen closely. I most definitely didn't. Most tomes had never been bibliomancers, and the ones that had didn't seem to care about stories or anything fun. They mostly seemed to gripe about arcane theories and one another. Boring old men, even the ones who had never been men.

Pliny pushed aside some space on a low table and sat me down. "Tell me what happened?" he asked and went about brewing some tea. I told him the whole thing, leaving out the part where I was mooning over my ex and telling stories to Ma because those weren't any of his business.

"How awful," he said, then handed me a tea and took the seat across from me.

I waited for him to take a drink of his tea before I sipped my own. You see, even back then I wasn't totally naive.

"Yeah, well, I've had worse." I hadn't. "But I can't figure out why they'd attack me, rather than just let me hand over the package."

"They might have been trying to cover their tracks," he said, and sipped his drink. "Or maybe they're just dumb. I mean, nothing about—what was it you called them?—fly cultists suggests cleverness."

"Good point. But I'd really rather not get killed by anyone that stupid, so I need your help."

"Of course," he said. "Anything. What do you need?"

"I need to know who ordered that delivery—what they looked like, how they signed for the delivery. I need to know who tried to kill me."

"I don't know how much I have recorded," he said, sadly. He noticed my expression. "Don't worry. I think I can help you. But I need you to promise me you'll let me give you all the details before you go off and get in over your head." I had to stop myself from tensing. What if things were even worse than I feared? Pliny didn't seem distressed, though. He sipped his tea casually.

"No problem," I said. "It's a little late in the evening for a rampage." I had to know. Without answers, I was good as Dropped.

"In a strange way," he said. "It doesn't really matter who sent the book. There have always been doomsday cultists among the lower classes—no offense. But you've seen it. People with nothing to lose start thinking the end of everything might work out well for them."

"That tome wasn't going to help them with that, though."

"No," he said. "Not in the way they thought, anyway. Whoever sent it was likely manipulating them. To get them to enact whatever ritual the tome contained."

"Wouldn't they see that coming?" I asked. "My—friend figured it out in ten minutes."

"The cultists? All they needed to do was get you inside without tipping you off, and they couldn't even manage that."

"Fair point," I said. "So, someone's trying to bait them into—what? Bringing about the end of the world?"

"Nothing so dramatic. Most gods want the world to continue—some variant of the world, anyway. They want to hold on to their power."

"So, what are they up to?" I asked. The knot in my gut was tightening.

"You've been all over this city, Danae. Does it seem like a good deal for most people? Like they're living good lives?"

I grunted and sipped my tea. I liked Pliny well enough, and more than that I needed answers, so I didn't tell him he didn't know much about what life was like farther out.

"The Lord Mayor profits, and his friends profit," he went on. "The Wise Ones play elaborate games against each other and Hishonor. And people starve."

"We manage," I said. "Mostly. I don't see what this has to do with the end of the world."

"I told you it's not the end, Danae." He brought his hands up expansively. "The toppling of the social order. Tearing down the towers of the powerful. Making everyone equal."

I looked around. There was more wealth in this room than in the whole of the outer web, if I guessed right. "Silly me," I said. "I'd settle for more water-collection vats."

He leaned forward. The pages that had been his hair parted down the middle. "I know you have more vision than that. Things will keep getting worse and worse. None of the powerful care a bit about us."

Oh. You're probably thinking, shit, took her long enough to be sure. Fair enough. But not many of us are ready the first time a friend tries to bring about an apocalypse. I pushed back from the table.

"And of course, whoever made the ritual possible would earn something from the Power they summoned, wouldn't they?"

"Well, yes," he said. "I would expect so."

"So, who was it?" I tried to think of who he'd want. "One of the Elder Lords? A Winter God?"

He laughed, finished his tea. "Nothing so banal. The Crafter herself."

I'd never been sure she was up there behind the moon. But even if he was wrong, *something* was coming if the ritual took place.

"This can't all be about—about leveling things," I said. "What do you want from her, Pliny?"

"Justice," he said, and stood up, flicking lint from his robes. "And she's the Crafter—she can put me back the way I was. Think of it, Danae! All the power without the, ahem, side-effects."

I shifted my weight. I didn't like thinking of the change that way, as if it was a curse. "Why are you telling me this?"

He sighed. "I thought it was obvious. I want your help. I know you have an—affinity with her. And you can't like the rich folk any more than I do. And of course, she might be able to help your mother."

Well, that brought me up short. I wasn't sure I believed in the Crafter or undoing transformations. But as much as I love Traverse, the web is no place for a tree. I could plant her in the garden, but even then ...

"The gardens," I said.

He'd picked up a book and was flipping through it. "What are you talking about?" I gauged the distance between us: no more than a meter. But bibliomancers were bad news. Given a well-chosen text to read from,

they could work magic more diverse than even the
greatest pictomancers, and of course I had no idea what
he was reading, so no way to prepare. That's when I
realized I was going to die.

"The gardens," I said sadly. "When the Crafter comes
back and takes control of her web, everything's coming
down. The gardens won't survive."

I watched his expression move from bafflement to
contempt. "There are always costs when things change,
Danae."

And I knew who would bear those costs. "Okay," I said.
"I'll hear you out. What's your off—" I lunged at him,
swinging hard at his jaw. I was fast. He was old. But I had
not caught him as off-guard as I'd hoped.

"Shield my steps," he blurted, and I hit hard into a wall
of energy. I staggered back and threw myself behind the
counter. Just in time.

"The foul betrayer is a poison," he shouted. I gagged.
The air fouled around me. So much for cover. I used the
counter for leverage and leapt to the far wall, where I
clutched the bookcase. It creaked and swayed ominously. He
turned to face me. I leapt again, sending books clattering
from their shelves. One of them shouted obscenities.

I didn't hear what Pliny said, but there was a flash of
light, a room-shaking explosion, and the bookshelf in front
of me was smoldering.

I pushed off, landed on the table—tea went flying—
and dove for his midsection. He sidestepped. Almost fast
enough. I clipped his shoulder, then hit the ground hard.
When I got my head up again he was struggling out of a
pile of books. He'd grabbed a new one.

"You're really galling me," he spat, and read. "Oh, the
spears of fate."

I really didn't want to be murdered by a cliché. Three
spears materialized, flying at my chest. I leapt and
clutched the ceiling, my fingers and toes holding fast.

I hadn't consciously called on that magic, but I'd called on it nonetheless. It had saved my life. For the moment.

I gathered myself for another attempt.

"You're a talented girl," he said. "But it's time you learned, 'everything breaks.'"

I heard the crack a moment before my brain decided to clue me in that a bone was jutting out from my arm. A moment later I was screaming in agony on the floor.

And what did that rutting mage do? Calmly rose to his feet and stood over me, tears in his eyes, while I was trying not to pass out. "I do so hate to waste promising materials," he said, and flipped through his book. "Trash, nothing but trash. Ah well. This will do—"

I wish I could tell you I had a good one-liner. But I was fighting against shock, and it was all I could do to call upon the power I'd been avoiding. Transformation is no curse.

I spat at him with all the contempt I could muster.

He blinked, then clutched his face, screamed, and fell back over the scattered books, landing hard. The scream's pitch kept rising and rising. He clutched at the ruins of his skin, thrashing wildly. Spiders have so many tricks, you see. I clutched my badly broken arm to my side and crawled over to him. It was an agonizing few feet, but I made it.

I didn't taunt him, and he didn't have a snappy line. His thrashing felt familiar to me. He felt like prey. I embraced my power, and bit hard into the soft skin of his leg. I felt the venom flow through my bite.

After a few minutes, the screaming stopped. Did his rich neighbors lift a finger to help? No rutting chance. It would take a while before he was soft enough. No matter. Despite the pain in my arm shooting white fireworks over the edges of my vision, I felt Traverse stretching out on all sides: The Lord Mayor asleep in his tower, a Wise One walking the streets incognito, merchants in finery eating imported delicacies, children playing on the edge of nothing. I felt my Ma, asleep, her green heart beating slowly.

I felt Socha, looking out over the night, their muscles tense. I felt the fly-cultists plotting in an abandoned house. Let them come for me. I would be ready.

I tore off Pliny's robes and fashioned a splint as best I could. Nearly passed out, but I managed to secure it. I had never felt more alive. As far as I was concerned, all the gods could take the Drop. But Pliny was right about one thing: Traverse was a mess. And, of course, every web needs its spider.

Pliny was prepared soon enough. When I was fully sated, I forced myself to my feet. The arm would need care, but I was owed a favor or two.

At the front door, I nodded to the orb spider, one equal to another. Then I went out into my city.

Hopper in
the Frying Pan

⟨ ◆⟩◆⟨◆⟩ ⟩

A S THE COP slams me to the hood of his car, I begin
to wish I'd paid more attention to who I am today.
He slaps cuffs on me but I don't start getting truly
worried until he reads me my rights and follows it up with
"we got you, you motherfucker."

From the ads that have been projected into my optics
since I woke up this morning (convoluted derivative
schemes, luxury cars, something called the Homeless
Hunting Simulator), I'd have figured my current Spoof for
some white-collar bullshit at most. But cops don't make
sure to bang a rich white dude's head against the car door
while taking him in for insider trading. We're winding
through the streets of Brooklyn when I get a notification
suggesting I contact the lawyer I have on retainer. But
since that's actually the lawyer my Spoof put on retainer,
I can't risk it. Too likely the lawyer knows this dude on
sight, and then I'm extra fucked.

So I do what little I can: I check my bots and dump the
whole file on my Spoof to the Hopper channel. Maybe
my Hopper crew can help me figure out what I—what
he—am supposed to have done. Outside the cop car,

the city flashes by, custom ads reading my presence and offering yachts and real-meat steaks and escort services, high-end shit as different as possible from the ads for antidepressants, crummy gigs and knock-off clothes I got before I started Hopping.

I try to ask the cop what this is about, but he gives me this look, pure hatred under a pair of bushy eyebrows, that shuts me right up. I'm confident he would beat the shit out of me if he thought he could get away with it. My only protection is also what's got me trapped: as long as I'm Jared Eric Pai Jr. the cops have to treat me like someone who could hurt them, and as long as I'm Pai, I'll be in their crosshairs.

THE THING ABOUT the internet is: it's not very cinematic. Okay, the top-level stuff can be, with high-end optics putting out fully 3-D reality-integrated video and some trust-fund kids even springing for nasal implants. And even the more widely available stuff, SmartBuddies keeping you company for a subscription fee, interactive film stadia, personal soundtracks, it's all very surface. Meant to keep you happy, or close enough. But the real work of the internet, the kind of stuff that makes it possible for a nobody like me to become some rich criminal or any of a few billion other people, that's still done on screens, mostly typed or via voice transcription, just like the dinosaurs used to do. Not much to see.

So when I tell you about the Hoppers, and about 13LemursInASuit, you can imagine us wherever you like: a fancy branded tea-house in some gentrified shithole, a seedy net cafe bouncing signals off a few thousand network nodes so everyone stays anonymous, a penthouse suite overlooking midtown, whatever suits you.

While you're at it, imagine me as whomever. Pick
a gender, write in your own, make me imminently
fuckable or loathsome as a glitching billboard. Same with
13LemursInASuit. They're whomever you want them to
be. You know as much about their "real" selves as I do,
anyway.

13 taught me how to do the really good stuff, the
backend shit that I'm sure as fuck not going to tell you
how to do. I'd sooner tell you the name on my birth
certificate. It's the stuff you only tell someone you really
trust, or really feel pity for. (Let's guess at 13's reasons
together, eh?)

We were chatting, text only, because what matters is
the code. I've told 13 that I can't live like this. Back then
I didn't have optics and I'd just been outed to my parents
via clickbait ("the one thing you must do if your child is
trans"). I couldn't escape the ads, and they're feeding on a
lifetime of history that I couldn't leave behind if I wanted
to, because thousands of corporations have access to data
on me, and that's not going away even when I change my
name and my pronouns, even if I bounce halfway around
the world.

"You can't be nobody," 13 said. "Even if you wiped out
enough data, they'd just start building it again."

"I know. I'm fucked."

If you prefer, pretend we had this convo on its own, not
while we're also busy trying to see who can deface the ads
projected on the Washington Monument to say "Needs
more balls."

"You're fucked," 13 told me. "So stop being you." And
they laid it out for me: everyone who exists is getting
watched, and ever since the Blockchain Apocalypse,
they're getting matched with data from the same
databases, getting sold to and sold off. You can't be
forgotten, so instead you become someone else.

Me: "Identity theft? They'd track me down instantly."

"Not instantly. Quick, though. You don't stay. You hop."

I was starting to get it. If you have to be somebody, keep being somebody new. By the time they start to figure out who you were, you're on to the next.

"But you're still leaving behind a pattern, biometrics, vid, all that."

I could almost hear them laughing. "And when they try to ID you, they'll turn up the record of whomever you're Spoofing."

I thought about this. "Fucks over that person pretty hard."

"Only briefly. If you cause enough trouble for them to get pulled in, before long their bio won't match."

That's when 13 introduced me to the Hopper channel, the folks who would become my real family, the one I chose. I learned a lot from them, and some of it I'm willing to tell you.

Here's what nobody explains when you're in your cradle and need to hear it: don't try to be somebody. And a corollary: The only way to be nobody is to be everybody.

I won the contest, by the way, and was particularly proud of my hand-crafted dildo animation removing what little subtlety there was in the Washington Monument's subtext.

THE INTERROGATION ROOM is brought to you by GoogleLaw, Cup Noodles, Ace Bail Bonds and Indenturing Agents, and the letters F-U-C and K. They've got tech to keep my optics from connecting to the outside world—might give me ideas about my rights. But they're happy to push ads at me for fancy-ass lawyers, meal-and-room upgrades, and medical care (at a substantial markup, naturally). Just because they've shut down my connection to the outside world doesn't mean they don't know who I am—don't know who Pai is.

The cops have nabbed a few of us Hoppers, over the years. Fortunately, They don't know there's such a thing as *us*, or we'd all be in hot shit, but they know they've caught some people Spoofing. And why do they get caught? Usually because they stay as some privileged shitstain for too long, or hop between 'em in a way anyone can see coming. You want to stay safe, you hop Spoofs at random, like I've been doing. At least, that's supposed to keep you safe. Over the years a few of us have gone missing, NeroHour and Switch2.1 and 8orAid. Is whatever happened to them coming for me? Not a comforting thought.

("I'm worried about them," I told 13 once.

"That doesn't help them. I'll keep looking. You keep yourself safe."

Did I stay up late into the night wondering if their interest was friendship or something more? Of course I did.)

Despite the cops' precautions, I'm using my optics to try to find a backdoor into the Police network—fuckers still aren't spending what they should on security—when the cops come storming in, Angry Eyebrows and his buddy, Unkempt Mustache, who shouts a lot and slams a folder down in front of me. He demands a confession. Another detective, female-presenting with an aggressive haircut, stands in the back of the room and watches silently. It's all pretty much what you'd see on any vidscreen, which gets me wondering whether cops always handled interrogations this way, or whether they picked it up from old shows, maybe getting nostalgic about old Miami and watching Sex Crimes South Beach or whatever.

I'm thinking about that and mostly ignoring their shit—easy, because anything I say will fuck me over hard. Whatever it is they think I've done, it's nothing compared to a few thousand counts of fraud, and a chance for the Feds to make an example of me, tear apart the Hoppers, and ruin the only bit of real freedom any of us have left.

(Can you imagine back in the day, when ads weren't aimed at you personally, weren't crafted to make every pleasure center in your brain light up? I don't have to imagine it, and it's *glorious*.) Anyway, I'm distracting myself because 1. I don't have options, 2. the first rule of dealing with cops is *never talk to the motherfucking cops*, and 3. I don't want to freak out.

Then the Mustache shows me the photos and I freak out. Full on jump up from my seat cursing, and trying to pull away from a table that of course I'm handcuffed to, because holy shitfuckers Mr. Pai, what did you fucking do?

I'm sure as shit not going to tell you what I saw, because even letting my mind drift back to it makes my gray matter want to claw its way free, but it was bad, and there was lots of it, and whoever did it was messed up on a scale I can't fathom.

Detective Mustache looks at me strangely, maybe trying to decide if I'm a good enough actor to have faked that reaction. I'm good, but not nearly that good. My real trick is confidence. That and contouring.

"We know you did it," he says. "What we want to know is why." Like I said: right out of the playbook. But now I'm seriously messed up because if they're right this Pai fuck has left a trail of bodies behind him, and my cultivated silence is in danger of cracking.

"Got nothing to say, tough guy?" he presses on. "Those girls, did they say anything?" I think I'm going to be sick. Sure, I hop between Spoofs, spend a little of some poor suckers credit, use their info to get into some parties I could never have imagined before. But even a little violence turns my stomach. And this—this is something new.

"I didn't do it," I say, breaking my rule.

"We've got your bio all over the scenes," he said. "You had to know we'd catch you. So tell me: why?"

That's shocked me back into silence, though. Even a rich fucker would get caught immediately leaving DNA at multiple murder scenes.

"Don't go all quiet on me now," he said. "I bet you're a real smooth talker, aren't you. You had to be, to talk them—"

But I've tuned him out again, mostly because if I hear him describe Pai's work I'm sure I'll vomit, and partly because that's what happens to me when I have a puzzle to sort out. Could Pai be a Hopper? I don't like to think one of us could be a serial killer, and even if one was, what are the odds that we just happened to be on this same Spoof? One thing's clear: he got away with this for a long time, and now it is linked to him, so something has gone seriously wrong.

The cops try more shouting, threats, kindness, whatever they can think of, but my thoughts are far away. Because now even if I can get myself out of this, this could blow back on the whole Hopper community, and they're the only family I've got left. They opened the world to me, saved my life, and that's a debt I can never repay.

IT TAKES ME a couple hours to crack the station's network, but what the hell, it's not like I could sleep if I wanted to. When I finally get online, hoping for help from the other Hoppers, and there's nothing. Complete silence. This *never* happens. I'm pretty messed up when a few moments later, a message comes in over a back channel. 12PlusPrimates: *Someone put a seriously nasty virus on that Pai file. I had to go to a backup account. Hang in there. Here's what little I know.*

There's a small file attached. It's not good news. 13 was able to dig up some records of the police investigation—I told you cop cybersecurity was shit—and Pai hadn't been fingered for those murders until a few weeks ago, and he hadn't shown on the grid at all since then. Before that, the DNA matches had been to a string of deceased people, as though the dead were committing each new crime. Pai's been stealing the dead's identities for a long time, and the fact that he isn't bothering anymore means he's either dead somewhere or up to something very bad. Pai's rich enough that he could be deep in hiding. Or, you know, about to frame someone for this shit. My chest tightens like someone drove a street-sweeper over it.

I need to get out of Pai's identities and out of here. My connection is throttled as fuck—I guess that's one way to keep cops from checking out porn at work—so I'm pretty limited in what I can do. Anyway, even if I bounce identities now, it won't do me any good, because they think they have Pai and they're not about to run those biometrics again. And given what Pai's done, they'll haul me before a judge in the morning, I won't make bail—I don't have access to enough of Pai's credit for a good lawyer, and can't use Pai's—and I'll get hauled off somewhere worse.

But I'm not totally out of ideas. I move a few hundred in CopCoin to a private account, activate my backup bot (something I can't place nags at me, saying I shouldn't use my primary), and message 13's backup account, asking them for one more favor.

I GET MAYBE an hour of dream-haunted sleep before they come to collect me. With no windows, I'm not supposed to know what time it is, but my optics, still connected to the local network, tell me it's ten before eight. They're in a fucking hurry to get me to court, and I'm sweating and thinking about what I'm gonna do if things don't come together.

Angry Eyebrows is loving this, telling me I'm going down for it, taunting me about what they'll do to me in prison, and it's clear he's already been bragging about this collar. I'm desperately hoping I'll be able to ruin his day.

But when they take me to a truck and load me in the back, and I'm pretty well fucked. I'm just about to start screaming about how they've got the wrong person, how if they just run my biometrics again I can prove it, which won't work, and would put every Hopper at risk. Somehow I keep my nerve, or at least keep my mouth shut, and outside I can barely hear raised voices. I'm hoping I'm the subject of debate, and sure enough a minute later they open the truck back up.

"What's going on?" I ask, trying to sound genuinely confused, and get pushed along roughly for my trouble. They take me to an intake room and give me another retinal scan. So 13 managed it after all. Eyebrows wants to take me back to the truck, but his sergeant tells him to wait. Seems they have a hot tip that my retinals will turn up additional outstanding warrants.

Still a million ways this can go wrong, but when the sergeant gets the results to her eye optics, it's easy to see it's gone right. She frowns, blinks, and her frown deepens. She pulls my cop aside.

"Run it again," I hear him say. And they do. Then they do two more biometric scans and another cross-check. They're fucking pissed, and I should win an Oscar for my portrayal of "confused inmate #1."

In the end they've got no choice but to apologize to me, or rather "Mr. Cory Cadigan," for the confusion. Seems Cadigan had an unpaid parking ticket and a warrant he didn't know about. I'm gracious, because I care more about getting clear of this than scoring points, and offer to pay the fine immediately. They're eager to get me out of there and try to figure out how their system pegged me as a serial killer.

Outside the station the ads are for vat-grown meat and child care and a helluva lot of prescription medications. Cadigan is more my type than Pai ever was. For about fifteen seconds, I think I'm in the clear. Then the other detective from the interrogation, Severe Haircut, is walking along side me.

"I know how you did it," she says, and I keep my head down and keep walking, my heart jittering. "I know you've been moving between identities, stealing them."

It's a one-sided conversation because of my "don't talk to the cops" rule, but that doesn't mean I'm ignoring her, and I don't dare start running.

"Fortunately for you," Haircut says, "I don't think you're a serial killer. Just some dumb kid in over his head." I guess I flinch at the pronoun, because she goes silent, then gives me a long look before continuing.

"You're going to want to hear what I have to say, 'Mr. Cadigan,'" she says, and pulls me into a nearby alleyway. I don't want to get shot in the back or arrested again, so what choice do I have? "Whatever you're up to, Pai is better at it than you are, and you've seen what he can do." She quirks a half-smile at my expression. "What you really need to think about is this: no way any of this happened by chance. You were set up, and now you know it.

"You're in a lot of danger. Once you decide I'm right, message me. I can help you." She taps her temple, and her VituaCard info splashes in front of my optics: Detective Laura Conrad.

She waits a few seconds, but I'm silent and probably look sick as fuck. She turns away, and I vomit against a nearby dumpster.

The more I think about it, the more I'm sure she's right. Had Pai somehow set things up so my random Hopping would end up on him? Has he infiltrated the Hoppers? He's certainly responsible for the virus that took out the Hopper channel.

I try to reach out to 13, but now even the backup line isn't getting through. Fuck all the ducks. I vomit again. Nothing but bile.

❧

I'VE GOT A place that more or less passes for home. Not that I'm there much. Really, it's just a flat where I can count on a mattress to flop on and roommates who don't ask questions. But I don't know what Pai knows, so I can't risk going there, and I find myself wandering the streets.

Ads flash around me, aimed at Cadigan, and they are easier to tune out than they've ever been, because I can't help but wonder if every half-hooded stranger, every man leaning casually in the shadows, is Pai. I can't think of anything better to do than be in extremely public places, so I head towards Prospect Park, lines of code running through my optics, trying to see if my suspicion is right. It's a warm morning, and the park is crowded with the unhurried rich, taking in optics-enhanced greens and dirty pigeons that look like brilliant doves as long as they stay within the park's boundaries. I'm too haggard to feel I can comfortably blend in, but I take a seat on a bench anyway, positioning myself to minimize the discomfort of the ribs and knobs meant to dissuade the homeless from sleeping here.

That's where I find what I'm looking for. I say "oh fucking shitballs" loud enough to draw angry glares, but for once I don't much care that my mask has slipped. My primary bot is programmed to generate a random number and query the server for the corresponding ID to Spoof. Works perfectly for keeping anyone guessing where I'm headed. Anyone but Pai, who spoofed the fucking server, intercepted my request, and sent me whatever identity he wants. If I hadn't followed my hunch and used my backup bot, I'd still be in jail. Pai's been tracking me for who knows how long, manipulating my very identity whenever he wants to.

Waves of terror wash over me. Is he watching me? How much does he know? Is he one of us, someone I thought was family? Or has he been stalking us, learning from us? To manage that, he'd have to have high-end tech—my brain is trying to process all this, as though I'm capable

of solving a logic puzzle while I'm this panicked. At some
point I realize I've stumbled out of the park and am
running through the streets of Brooklyn, no idea where
I'm going.

When I finally stop to catch my breath, I finally start
noticing the ads again, and holy shitkickers: the message
my optics show on the brownstone wall opposite me?
Keep running, little bird. I like the chase. I'm so freaked out
that I barely notice the mixed metaphor. I whirl around
frantically, but I don't see anyone staring, and there's
no way to know if he's physically present or tracking me
virtually. Not until he's ready to make sure I end up like
all those women.

And there, on the corner where some ultra-rich
redevelopment is in the process of cannibalizing the last of
the old neighborhood, it hits me. Pai's been using Hopper
tools against us. We've been his targets. Those murders
the cops were so eager to show me? My friends. My
fucking family. NeroHour, Switch, 8, probably others too.
And I'm vomiting again, dry heaving over and over, while
I sob angry, desperate tears.

When I'm able to catch my breath, I desperately send
another round of messages to the group, trying to warn
them, but every one bounces back. Pai has me locked
away from the Hoppers. I'm all alone. And once he kills
me, what's to stop him from preying on them again,
maybe even while wearing my name?

The ad across the way flashes to life: *No night too rough for
OxyMints.* I hear myself trying to scream, but I can't seem
to find the air.

Eventually I start walking, because I'm too tired to run,
and too terrified to stay in one place. It seems like every
fifth ad is from Pai: *Run, run, run, fast as you can, or you'll look
beautiful cut open.* Not subtle. Like a lion closing in on its prey.

To my surprise, that thought steadies me. Tugs at the
back of my brain. The male lion wants you to know he's

there, wants you to be terrified, distracted. So the trap the females have set can spring on you. I've been falling for it, like some dumbshit tourist buying all the ad space on the Brooklyn Bridge.

I need time and space to think, to plan. But those are luxuries I don't have. I get my bearings, then head toward the library branch in Park Slope. While I'm walking, I code, talking quietly to myself and ignoring the strange looks of passersby. I pay my library access fee—sorry, Cory Cadigan, for what's probably going to put a big dent in your budget—and make my way to an access terminal. The secondary fee isn't so bad, and now I can work in relative safety until the library closes.

Pai knows where I am. When I leave here, I'm going to die.

IT'S WELL AFTER dark when they announce closing time. I forced myself to sleep for an hour, mainly to get away from the relentless stream of threatening ads Pai's been sending my way. It's nowhere close to enough sleep, and I wonder if I'm going to die having slept less than two hours in two days.

A few minutes before closing, I run the program I've written, and pray to all the gods that my guess on timing is right. Too soon and I'll be back in jail and at the cops' (or Pai's) mercies. Too late and I'll be dead.

I wait until a security guard kicks me out. From the rough way he handles me, it's pretty clear he enjoys throwing out homeless or otherwise desperate people. I'm certainly more than desperate enough to qualify, and I'm hoping that Pai will see me as completely lost to panic, and that might give me a bit of an edge. I need every break I can get.

I stand on the street-corner outside the library. The neighborhood is well-lit, but the streets are practically empty. The buildings around me are full of people rich enough to mind their own business. None of them are coming to help me. I'm looking back and forth, none of my fear faked, when the limo pulls up. Long and black, it's the kind of vehicle that exists only to show off its own impracticality. The backdoor slides open soundlessly.

"Get in the car, K1tBash," says a voice from inside. I do my best not to let on that I'm relieved: I knew Pai knew my handle. That he didn't use my given name gives me hope that he doesn't know everything about me.

I hesitate for a long moment, both because I'm terrified and because I'm trying to show it, then climb into the car. The door slides shut behind me and locks. Pai sits in shadow opposite me, cosmetic optics in his eyes causing them to glow red. I imagine those eyes gleaming as he murdered my friends, and for a moment my fear shifts into hatred.

"Oh, she's an angry one, isn't she?" His voice is low and mocking, absolutely confident. I'm such a mess the pronouns barely register.

"What do you want?" I ask, because I don't trust myself to say anything else.

He laughs cruelly, and orders the car's AI to take him to an address I don't recognize. I try to query it through my optics, but of course he's blocked them. A sharper panic flows through me for a moment, but outside the ads shift as we drive by—apartments for rent, home brewing equipment, fertility treatments—and I know my optics are still being read by the ad network, that I still have a shot.

"You killed my friends," I say. "Why?"

His teeth flash and he leans forward. He's tall, muscled in a way that suggests he's paid for subdermal enhancements, but his temples are graying. He looks like any generic exec, which I suppose is the point.

"I'm doing the world a favor," he says, "cleaning up trash like you." But I can see the hungry gleam in his eyes.

"This isn't about justice," I say, my voice shaking with rage or anger. "I've seen the photos."

"Trash like you can't appreciate true beauty," he says. "But don't worry, filth. I'll make you beautiful." He cracks his knuckles loudly. What the actual fuck.

"Why me?" I ask, my voice shaking. I don't have any real hope of learning anything from his words, but stomach-grinding as they are, silence is somehow worse.

He's happy to talk, of course. I'd always heard serial killers were dysfunctional loners, but this dude put his money, charm, and expertise into it. He's happy to share in horrid detail his "favorite hobby." I'll spare you. It's enough to know that I'm grateful there was nothing left in my stomach. The only part that really matters is this, and he's oh-so-happy to make sure I know it: when I'm dead, he'll move on to the next of us: "I could pin it all on you, but I think I'll start over with a new identity. No reason artists should give up their calling." And, I shit you not, he licks his fucking lips.

I have nothing to say to that. The car pulls into some darkened garage. He produces a gun; it doesn't matter. There's no more running. We're both where our choices brought us. Fuck.

I climb out of the car to find his little lab, antiseptic, with good drainage. I won't give him the pleasure of describing the details. They're horrifying, designed to help him torture and murder me. I wonder if he'll display my body, when he's done, or if he'll bother make it look like an accident? I doubt it, after what I saw in the photos. And the scene gives rise to a question I can't escape: am I standing where my friends died?

I can't help myself. I ask him.

"Cuff your hands to the chain above your head," he demands, "and I'll tell you." I contemplate rushing him, but he's the one with the gun, and his tech-supported reflexes are sure to be better than mine. I do as he asks, and he answers: "Of course not, you pathetic wretch. A new place every time. This one I'd been saving for someone special, but since the cops screwed up, I suppose you'll have to do."

He pulls out a knife. There are no ads anymore, nothing but me and him and the dungeon his money has bought him. I tell myself I'm not going to scream, but of course I'm screaming before the first cut.

His blade makes a series of fine lines across my arms, my chest, so sharp they hurt less than I expect.

"Don't worry," he says. "We're going to take our time, you and I."

The door shatters and floodlights poor in. I'm half-blind in the sudden light, so I get only vague impressions: Pai's mouth a shocked "O," his hand raised, the blade above it. Shots ring out, echoing through the room like the rawest screams.

I WAKE UP in a hospital bed, my ears still ringing from the blasts. Severe Haircut—Detective Conrad—is sitting in the chair next to mine, and says something. It doesn't cut the ringing, so I point to my ears. She seems to get the idea, holds up one finger, and leaves the room.

By the time she returns a few minutes later with two cups of coffee, I've been able to assess the situation. I'm not hurting as badly as I expected to be, my wounds arc bandaged, and the machines are telling me my vitals are okay. Also, I'm not handcuffed to the bed, which is the best fucking news I've had all day. Well, second best, after waking up alive.

She hands me a coffee and I take a sip. It burns going down, but in a good way.

"How're you feeling?" she asks me. I just grunt. "We're going to need a statement from you," she says, smiling.

"Am I under arrest?" I ask.

"No," she admits. "But you're the primary witness—"

"Am I free to go?"

"Not until the hospital discharges you."

I frown and clam up.

"Don't be difficult," she says, still friendly. "We could charge you for identity theft, fraud, and impersonating a police officer, at minimum."

I remember my rules, and don't say shit.

"Hmmm," she continues. "You were clever. I have to admit that. I'm guessing you knew he was monitoring your communications, so you didn't try to reach me directly, just snagged my identity. I went ahead and canceled the order you made for, ahem, several hundred dollars in pork rinds and donuts." She's got this look on her face like she wants to be impressed but isn't sure she should let herself be.

I remain stone-faced. "Well," she says, "and here I thought we were friends." She stands up. "You know how to reach me, if you change your mind."

She starts out of the room and, fuck it, I just can't resist. "Pai?" I ask, and she turns around grinning.

"I thought you'd never ask. He's been in surgery for several hours, but even if he makes it, the doctors tell me the brain damage will be extensive."

I must visibly relax, because her grin widens as she watches me. "Lucky for you, I'm not particularly interested in complicating the biggest collar of my career with your petty bullshit. But when you're out of the hospital, I suggest you get out of town. The investigation will turn up something on you sooner or later."

I know she's right, and anyway I'd already decided it's time to go. I'm fucking sick of New York anyway. And, hell, this is the best-case scenario for dealing with the cops: they let you walk away, this time.

I nod, but don't say anything else, and Conrad heads out. I call for the nurse, and by the time he arrives, I'm already dressed and sorting through the avalanche of messages from the other Hoppers. Seems they're back online.

"Have I got a story for you," I send them. 13 sends me an image: a single heart. I feel a flutter in my stomach that has nothing to do with fear. I've got scars on my arms and chest, and emotional scars that will take a lot more treating. That's all trauma I'll need to work through. Later. For now I need to share everything I learned with the people I love.

By the time I'm out of the hospital, I've already queued up a new identity, but I don't even notice the ads. Sure, someday my luck may run out, but for now I'm free. Can you say the same, out there, being whoever it is they've told you to be?

Blades, Stones, and the Weight of Centuries

EVERYTHING DEPENDED ON Princess Marah's ability to
sit upon the Great Throne.

The heart of the empire, it rested at the pinnacle
of the Grand Pyramid. Though she was heir to the
Millennial Empire, Marah could only approach the
throne cautiously.

Around her in every direction stretched the grid-lines
of Millennium, the capital city, yet she was alone, save
for the two tongueless guards who stood at attention. The
afternoon sun was descending in the west, behind the
smoke that rose from the distant hills. One could almost
forget that the armies of the Emperor worked even now to
root out the rebels. Marah gritted her teeth, adjusting her
posture the way the courtiers had taught her, and resisted
the urge to shift her weight to calm her nerves. Such
things were unbecoming a princess, and if she couldn't
master them, she would never be able to sit on the throne.

Marah forced herself to step closer. The throne's sharp,
unyielding lines curved only slightly from the indentations
of generations of imperial rulers. Her father should have
been here to oversee the day's petitioners, but he was ill,

bedridden, and now his last living child needed to learn to sit in his stead. She took one more step, then two. The throne hummed with the power of countless generations who had labored to build the pyramid, securing the might of the empire for all time, or so it was said. There was no doubt that the magic of uncountable specialists, craftspeople, petromancers, architects, warriors, and servants had each shaped the power before her. What was Marah compared to that? Who was she to believe she was fit to rule?

Another step forward. Marah could feel the throne's magic pushing at her, inquiring, deciding if she was worthy. Tentatively, she reached out one soft hand. The throne, reluctant, held her at bay with an invisible force.

"It will never accept you until you force it to, your highness," said a voice from behind her. She did not turn to face the captain of her father's guard, willing herself to hold her composure. She was sure he had his own plans, should her father fail to secure a proper union for her.

"So you've said, Perroh," Marah said and turned to face him. He'd entered the throne room silently, no doubt hoping to embarrass her. *You are heir to the throne,* she told herself. *You will comport yourself with dignity.* She could practically hear her tutors' voices in her ear. "But I will not be lectured by you. While my father is indisposed, he has commanded that I speak with his voice."

Perroh stood more than a head taller than her and kept his hand on the hilt of his blade in a way that radiated danger. He'd killed no fewer than five would-be regicides, and before that won acclaim battling the forces of the spider-city in the lands far to the southwest. His vest still displayed his general's stars, though he was now officially retired to the relatively quiet life of her father's personal guard. Beneath his wiry beard, he wore a smirk, and Marah knew she had misstepped. A ruler who needs to remind others to respect them has no respect. Certainly,

the way his gaze traveled over the silken folds of her dress
proved that well enough.

"As my princess says," Perroh responded, not bothering
to conceal his grin, nor his eyes roving over her body.
He shrugged his bare shoulders, muscles rippling. Every
move he made was about power, she reminded herself, just
as every move her father made was. Just as the pyramid
and the empire had stayed strong for so long, because the
pyramid perfectly represented the empire's strength. "Will
you be seeing your petitioners here"—his eyes moved to
the throne—"or in the steward's chamber?" A challenge,
and one she could not answer while the throne rejected
her. She hesitated, his smile growing.

"I will see them here," she said impulsively, and was
rewarded with his face falling. But it would be a short-
lived victory. He'd soon know she could not sit on the
throne. She'd never been intended to, though she was
clever and a keen observer of others, though tutors called
her *willful*. None of that mattered, for she was the youngest
child, and a girl beside. But her eldest brother had died
putting down the Forest Rebellion, and her middle
brother had been consumed by vengeance and embraced
the magic of a pestimancer. He was no longer anything
one could recognize as a person. Even with their loss,
she would have avoided this fate, had she not rejected
her father's hand-picked suitors. If she'd just settled for
well enough, she would have been married off and ruling
would have been her husband's problem.

Husband. The word made her stomach knot. One
more reminder of the ways in which she was ill-suited to
her role.

Embrace the monarch-magic, her tutors told her. *Grasp its
power, and you will rule unquestioned.* That was the only way
to do powerful magic. Cantrips and such could be cast by
anyone, but if you wished to truly master a field of magic,
you had to fully embrace it. Transformation was the price

of that mastery. The most powerful emperor to ever live, Zaneth the Second, her thrice-great grandfather, was said to have eventually become one with his throne. She must be Emperor someday, and her body would re-shape itself to the needs of the throne, of the pyramid, the Empire. That was her fate, whether she wanted it or not.

When Perroh left to retrieve the first petitioners, she practically threw herself at the throne, desperate to be seated in full authority when he returned. It batted her away like she was a gnat. Neither of the guards reacted as she picked herself up, her cheeks burning.

OVERSEEING PETITIONS WAS only slightly less monotonous with Marah on the throne than standing beside it as her father dispensed judgment. "On the throne" was wrong, of course—she still stood, but in front of it, counting on her much-practiced regal bearing to make this seem a deliberate choice, though Perroh's smirk grew as the proceedings went on. She settled a few minor disputes and had the distinct impression that the claimants were happy to be facing her rather than her father.

All were happy but one: the last of the petitioners in line, a young woman with grey eyes, her cheekbones and chin so sharp that Marah half-wondered if she would cut herself against them. A shiver ran down Marah's back, but she pushed the treacherous thought away. The woman wore moth-eaten robes, and her jaw was tenser than a coiled serpent. She watched Marah with a focus that unnerved the princess. Throughout the petitions, her eyes were nearly constantly on Marah's face, only occasionally glancing elsewhere in the room. It was not the nakedly possessive gaze of Perroh, nor the disappointed glare of her father. It was...what?

Marah shivered, and pressed on with her duties, until of the petitioners, only the woman with the iron-grey eyes remained. She rose to her feet in one easy motion (not a spring, but a wild beast, Marah thought, far too late) and raised her left hand. It elongated even as she moved, jutting from her until it gleamed, long and sharp, a blade.

She rammed it through the first guard before his hand had even reached his pommel, up under a gap in his chainmail and into his chest. The other guard drew his weapon and offered a wordless cry. Where his sword met what had been her hand, the room echoed with the clash of blades.

She spun away and he turned to face her—much too slowly. One slash at his heel and he was down; his armor sheared through, he would never rise. They had been talented guards, but this woman was something else, practicing a type of magic Marah had never seen, and doing so with deadly ease

The sword-woman's attention settled on Perroh, deadliest warrior in the kingdom, who hadn't yet entered the fight, but only stationed himself between the woman and Marah. For a horrifying moment, she feared they were working together, but then he drew his sword.

"You're good, gladiomancer," he said, casual arrogance in his voice. "But I am war embodied. Time to die."

The killer responded by leaping at him, her sword-arm flashing orange in the fading light. His own blade, broader and heavier than hers, rose to meet her, and then the two combatants engaged.

Marah had been taught the magic of a noblewoman, small tricks to command a household, to support her husband, and then, when she was still unmarried and had become the heir, the magic of the monarch. She had not even been allowed into the yard to watch the warriors train, even if she had snuck there from time to time to watch them with an avid but uninformed eye.

None of that had prepared her for this fight, which was to that sparring as the Grand Pyramid was to the laborers' shacks in its shadow. Their sword-work was too fast for her to follow, all feigns, testing blows, and nearly-decisive strikes. Perroh was half-a-head taller, and much stronger, but his foe was faster, with flowing moves and elegant footwork, and she consistently threatened his flanks even as he tried to force her into a corner.

Time was on Perroh's side, though—sooner or later other guards, stationed below, would realize something was wrong and come to offer reinforcements. At any time he could call for their aid, though he had not yet done so. Despite her contempt for him, Marah was certain she was watching Perroh finish off an outmatched foe. Slowly but undeniably he was closing off space, giving her fewer options. Marah stood transfixed, finding herself conflicted, as Perroh forced the woman between the throne and the room's back wall. The throne's bulk limited her options. She saw the trap, ducked as if to move under him, then side-stepped as his knee came up to meet her, vaulting over the throne with her off-hand. For a moment she seemed frozen in mid-air, the muscles in her arm flexed, until she rolled up and over as Perroh's blade impacted against the immortal stone of the throne.

His blade ricocheted and caught the sword-woman's arm. She grunted and tumbled forward—even as the throne pushed her away from it—straight at Marah. The two women had the briefest of moments to recognize what was coming, and then the gladiomancer twisted, clipping the princess's shoulder. Both went sprawling, Marah at the foot of the throne and the swordswoman a meter past her.

Perroh rushed forward, aiming to strike the killer's head from her shoulders, but she rolled away. His blade bit into the floor, missing her by centimeters. Blood slicked the stone beneath where she had fallen. She raised her blade-arm to stab at Perroh, but he swatted it away with contemptuous ease. He stood above her, raised his sword for the killing blow—

—as she drove the pointed fingertips of her other arm into his foot.

He gasped and tried to wrench himself free, but she leaped up, her sword driving upward under his chin and through his skull.

He blinked three times, the O of his mouth forming a word that might have been "how," before toppling backwards. She fell in a heap with him, then yanked her blades from his body.

"You were a warrior," she said, and spat. "I'm a blade." Then she grimaced, her dagger becoming fingers again, the blood from her wound mixing with Perroh's. She flexed them twice—the tips were gray against her blood, her dark skin—and put her sword to Marah's throat.

"Where is the Emperor?" she demanded. Marah's stomach twisted. She pressed back against the base of the throne. Or tried to. Still it kept her at a distance.

"He is…indisposed, and heavily guarded," she whispered. "You'll never get to him."

Drip-drip-drip, the blood from the sword-woman's arm pattered onto the stone floors of the pyramid. "You're the princess." It wasn't a question, just an observation. She hesitated, then seemed to resign herself to what she would do. "This isn't personal. I'm just a weapon."

Something in the way she said it tugged at Marah's thoughts. Her determination, her certainty. *Just a weapon…*

"I know you," she said, the realization hitting her with force. "You were one of the boys who trained in the yard."

The blade-woman pulled back as if Marah had struck her. She looked down and away. It was Marah's chance to flee. Instead, she pulled herself slowly to her feet.

"You were in training to be a guard," she said. She was sure of it now: that boy's face had been rounder, his body holding none of the war-forged lines the woman now possessed. But she remembered him even so, his refusal to stop, no matter how many times he was knocked down.

Or *she* was knocked down? Marah was unsure.

"How dare you remember?" the woman hissed, and raised her blade again, putting it against Marah's chest.

"You made an impression," Marah said. "And maybe I was jealous."

"Of what?" the woman said, glaring at her with such fury that Marah wondered if even her gaze could cut. The thought scared her, but not unpleasantly.

"Of the way you never quit. I've never wanted anything as badly as you wanted to be a guard."

She scoffed, glanced at her blade. "Look where that got me." But her fury had subsided. She took a deep breath, seeming to come to a decision. "Sit on the throne."

Marah blinked, confused, and tried again to sit. The throne pushed her away like she was an unwanted pet.

The other woman stared, her face twisting. "It doesn't want you," she said. "It rejected you. Why?"

Marah felt the glow in her cheeks but chose to ignore it. She stood, careful of the blood-slick floor. "I don't want to be Emperor." It was the first time she'd said it, and speaking the words made them feel real. Her knees shook.

"You don't, do you?" The swordswoman's bloody hand clenched with a sound like silverware clattering and she swore violently. "So, what do you want?"

Still no sound of guards coming from the lower levels. Marah could hear the ringing of steel from the training-yards below. Perroh hadn't bothered to call for help. They were alone.

"Do you still call yourself—" she started, but the other woman interrupted.

"Edge," she said. "My name is Edge."

Marah had never known one could use magic to change their gender, but then she'd never desired any path strongly enough to truly understand its magic. Edge wore the change as comfortably as she wore the sword.

"You really are a blade, aren't you?" Marah asked.

She'd drawn herself up to her full height, still well shorter than her attacker, but the other woman was clearly no longer certain what to do, which Marah understood all too well.

"Yes," Edge said. "I've trained for years for this. To kill your father." She said it with defiance, but Marah didn't rise to the bait. Edge had always wanted to use a blade, but what had changed to make her embrace so much gladiomancy? Already her fingers were becoming steel. How long would it be before she was fully subsumed by her own magic, before she was a blade entire?

"Why do you want to kill him?"

"In case what they say is true, that the king and his kingdom are one."

"You want to destroy the Empire?" Marah was shocked. "Why?"

Edge looked at her with pity. "He has no right to rule us."

Dominion is its own proof of rightness, Marah's tutors would have said. And: *The Empire thrives as the Emperor does.* But Marah hadn't seen much of the kingdom—she had never even been down to the lowest levels of the pyramid. *Traveling the lower levels would be unbecoming.*

How did the empire thrive? What had driven a loyal guard-in-training to attack at its heart?

"You could kill me, and my father would be without an heir," Marah said. Part of her said, *what a foolish thing to say.* And another part, *trust your instincts.* That second part did not come from her tutors. Whence had it come?

"I could," Edge said. She hesitated, then pulled her blade away from Marah's throat.

"But you won't," Marah said. "Why?"

"I should," she said, and paused for a long moment. "But I thought you were a collaborator. Now I see you're caught up in this, too."

The blood from the stones had crept up Marah's cream-colored gown, the embroidery at the hem now rust-red.

"Tell me," Marah said, and crossed the distance to look into Edge's eyes. "Let's say you succeed, that you kill him. What would you put in his place?"

Edge showed her teeth, defiant. "Others have plans for the future. I'm just a blade. And I want to shatter this pyramid."

Marah gasped. "But it would be carnage! Thousands of people live here, not just royalty. There are those who live in its shadow, and the workers—"

"You don't know anything about the workers." Edge turned her back on her, went to one of the windows. The sunset cast the city below in red light.

"You nobles are always the same," she went on. "So concerned with the cost of change, and not at all with the cost of carrying on."

The words lingered.

"They've never let me out to see," Marah admitted. "What cost do you mean?"

Edge grunted dismissively, hesitating, then turned around. She studied Marah's face, a look so frank and appraising it made the princess feel as though the room was spinning. What was this flutter in her throat?

"Come with me to the lower levels and I'll show you."

The pyramid was the physical embodiment of the monarch's power, towering, ever-expanding, unshakable. Those who sought the presence of the Emperor walked up and up the grand stairs on the east side. But those were not the only stairs. The pyramid was also the capitol, and there were passages for servants, and secret ones for the Emperor's spies, and others—so Marah had heard—to take one down into the dungeons, in the heart of the structure, where those went who would never again emerge. Marah knew some of the pathways, even though she had never taken them.

"I'll come with you," she said. "But first, I need to see to your wound." She unwrapped the ribbons that looped gracefully around her waist. They'd serve well enough as a temporary bandage.

She was rewarded with the sight of Edge's shocked expression.

◊

DEEP WITHIN THE pyramid's depths were hallways and chambers on which the sun had not shown since the early days of the Empire, the rough stone blocks of their walls were cool to the touch even now, in the heart of summer. They moved quickly, though there had, as yet, been no shouts of alarm from above, and likely would not be until another pair of guards arrived to take their brethren's place. The two women had managed to find their way more easily than Marah had dreamed. After a few levels, she'd been forced to guess at which path to take, but she had not yet steered them wrong.

"You're not the Emperor, but you are royalty," Edge had whispered. "The pyramid knows you, makes itself known to you."

Perhaps it was so, for they only once encountered another soul, a scullery maid who no doubt knew these tunnels far better than Marah could hope to. The woman gasped in surprise, and Edge hesitated, her blade poised, but didn't strike. The maid lifted her lantern, and regarded the two women; she was afraid, but did not cower.

"Shatter the stones," she said, and Edge lowered her blade-arm, leaving her to pass.

"What was that?" Marah hissed.

"Someone else the Empire has wounded," Edge said. Marah began to work to remember the maid's face, then thought better of it, and worked instead to forget it.

"The going would be easier if you, ah, *ungrew* your sword," she said.

"I'm...not sure I can." Edge stared at her blade.

"I'm sorry," Marah said. "I didn't realize—"
She stopped herself. Was Edge so far along in her
transformation that the blade was a permanent part of her?

"It doesn't matter." Edge's gaze hadn't left her weapon.
"My work's almost done."

It seemed Edge expected to die today. Marah could
think of nothing to say.

They went in silence to the depths, the wind whistling
around them. Marah hesitated. The wind? They were far
from the surface.

"What is that sound?" she asked at last.

"The wailing," Edge said. "The cries of the spirits in
the stones." She struck a match against her blade, lighting
a nearby brazier, so that the halls around them became
illuminated. The ancient walls of the pyramid seemed to
writhe in the light.

No. They *did* writhe. Their surfaces flowed with the
faint outlines of hands, of faces, mouths which opened as
if to scream and then faded back into the rock. Marah
stumbled back into the wall behind her, and felt a scream
tearing its way free—

Edge clamped her hand over Marah's mouth.
"Silence," she demanded, and the scream died in Marah's
throat. Edge's body threw off welcome heat, unlike the
chill radiating from the walls.

"What—how?" Marah managed.

"How do you think?" Edge said, and her voice seemed
more bitter than a fouled well. "Servants who worked
their whole lives shaping the stone, cutting and placing
it, building this monument to another man's power...what
magic do you think they used to do it?"

Marah said nothing. The answer was obvious. The
workers' sweat and blood mixed with the mortar between
stones. Day and night, they hauled, carved, breathed
stone. Day and night, it was their labor that held the

pyramid together. That was another kind of magic. And what was the fate of all mages?

"The builders..." was all the princess managed.

"Not all of them," Edge said, "but many." There was a hitch in her voice, something personal.

"I've never heard this before," Marah said. "The moaning. Stone everywhere. How——?"

"Other magic, no doubt," Edge said. "These are rough-cut stones, closer to their true essence. It wouldn't do to have royal guests see such a thing."

Marah stood staring, haunted by the stones, the only stability she'd ever known. "Your father—he was a laborer..."

"Yes," Edge's voice was sharp with pain. "Now you see. We have to end it, bring it down." She reached out, running one of her fingers along the battered surface of the wall. "Stone by stone if necessary."

"I didn't know..." Marah whispered. She sank to her knees. "Oh, Edge, I'm so sorry——"

"You're not responsible for that," Edge said quietly. "Only for what you do now that you do know."

"What can I do?"

"I'm glad you asked," Edge said, and inclined her head towards Marah. "We start by—what—" she paused, turned back, tugging at the wall. Her hand wouldn't come free. Stone encased her fingers, climbed toward her wrists. Furious forms moved over the rock's surface. "What is this? I'm trying to free you——"

The stone-forms ignored her, crawling upward as the two women looked on in horror. "Princess," Edge said, a plea cut short as she hacked uselessly at the stone. Her steel rang out against the moaning walls.

Why would trapped spirits of stone not wish to be released? And then Marah knew, just as she knew that many of her servants would not support Edge, even if it meant they never again had to use their own magic in the service of another.

"Some of them don't want to be freed," she said.

"What?" Edge said, wide-eyed. The stone was up nearly to her elbow and climbing up her boots. It meant to encase her.

Marah saw it all clearly now. What would it be like, to give your life to the building of a thing and have it destroyed? Even if the thing wasn't for you, even if it cost you everything, it imposed an order on the world, a purpose, a sense of shape. Not all of the stone-ghosts would see it that way, but some might. Edge thought the stones would choose freedom over bondage, but some had chosen this fate for themselves, or preferred it to alternatives. Was it so strange that they might choose the burden they knew to the unknown fate that followed being shattered?

The swordswoman opened her mouth as though to scream, but no cry came out, just a series of gasps as the stone swallowed her knees and upper arms.

"No," Marah said, finally finding movement in her limbs. "No." She rushed to Edge, put a hand to her cheek. The rebel watched her, her face a rictus. "No, this isn't right. You have to stop this! Stop it stop it *stop*—"

Marah paused, gathered herself. Crying and screaming would get nowhere and denying her position wouldn't save Edge. There was only ever one power these halls responded to.

"I am Marah, Crown Princess of the Thousand-Year-Empire," she said, pulling herself to her full height. Her hand was slick with Edge's tears. "You will release her."

A hesitation. Neither woman dared breathe.

"Now," Marah said, her voice cold.

The stone fell away.

Edge nearly fell. Marah caught her, staggering under the swordswoman's weight, but didn't fall. Edge gripped Marah tightly, the flat of her blade cold against the princess's back.

Around them, the stones thrummed with power.

Marah could feel it now; the power of the Grand Pyramid accepted her, called to her, rushed over her with a wave of welcome. It responded to her will, but also shaped it. The tower wasn't her, but it was hers, and she was its. Her thoughts spun with the good she could do with this power. It need not be a force for evil. She would stop new construction, make certain no more people ended as these stone-smiths had done. She would—

"You saved me," Edge said, still in her arms. "You used your magic and you saved me." She blinked back tears. Her steel fingertips were soft as whispers against the princess's cheek. Only as they came away wet did Marah realize that she, too, had been crying.

This close, Marah could see that Edge had thin white scars on each cheek, like the fine cuts of a sharp knife. She was shaking, strong and vulnerable in Marah's grasp.

"I thought I was ready to die," Edge said. "But not like that."

Marah leaned closer, until their faces were inches from one another. The whispers of the stones called to her, both those in agony and those who had attacked Edge.

"Thank you," Marah whispered, her eyes locked with Edge's.

"For what?"

"For helping me realize what I want." Marah could feel the smile curling at her lips. But she couldn't forget the grim expectation she'd seen in Edge's eyes. "I need you!" She blurted. "The world needs you! There's so much to do..."

"You don't need—" Edge shook her head. "Like I said, I'm a blade."

"Yes. But that's not all you are."

Edge bit her lip. Marah could feel the swordswoman's breath on her lips.

"Will you—kiss me?" Marah asked.

Edge's tear-bright face broadened into a smile. "Yes," she said. "Yes, please!"

Their lips met. The two women pulled apart, stared wordlessly at one another, and rejoined the kiss. Edge's tongue flicked at Marah's lips, which parted for her. Behind her, she felt the cold edge of the blade shift and change until it was no more, and two hands clutched her back, pulled her in more tightly, with a hint of cool steel to accompany their warmth.

Around them, the walls shivered and cracked. In his room, the King coughed violently, tossing in disturbed sleep. Far away in the hills, the battles continued. The pyramid was old magic, the Empire even older. Edge couldn't take down work of a thousand years by herself. Neither could Marah, no matter how much she wished to.

But then, they weren't alone. And even the greatest work had to start somewhere.

Those were thoughts for later. In that moment, in the heart of the Empire they meant to tear down, the two women thought only of each other.

III.

The Grass Bows Down, the Pilgrims Walk Lightly

MY MOTHER KEPT an old faith, and when I was young she would tell me stories of the Aesir. She explained how, each day, Odin sends his ravens into the world. Huginn and Muninn, Thought and Memory, scour the globe for what they may learn. Perhaps they will help him uncover the secret to preventing Ragnarök, the death of all he has worked to build. Until the ravens return, the god sits motionless as a statue. For without them, what is he?

WE CREST THE ridge, and the grasslands stretch to the horizon, each lavender blade as tall as my shoulder. The wild fields ripple in the wind, mottled by cloud-shadow. If I could, I would stay and watch the light and dark play over the wilderness, but Korvach starts down the slope immediately, and I must hurry to keep up. I am the guest of honor, or possibly the subject of a trial. Behind us extends a line of Klevish pilgrims.

Once or twice I have looked back to see dozens of them, dressed in slate-gray robes, their angular faces dominated by protrusions that strike me alternatively as a nose or a raven's beak, though they are neither. The effect of the whole is to make them seem like a line of plague doctors. An ominous association, but they have been polite and welcoming in their formal way.

At the bottom of the ridge, the rocky soil gives way to rich grassland. Korvach turns to me, though he does not break his stride. "You commune with us, Erika-Negotiator, by joining our pilgrimage. Now you may see something you have never seen before."

The briefing documents I'd read commented on the Klevish tendency toward understatement and noted that it was "most pronounced among devotees of the Known Path." Even so, I am not prepared for what happens. Korvach gestures casually with his hand and before us, the grass bows down.

There is no other way to describe it. The stalks all around sway gently in a light breeze, but the ones right in front of us each bend at the tuft that makes up the base of the blade and lie flat before us.

"We begin," Korvach says as he steps forward. For yards before each footfall, the grass in front of him ripples and bends down. We walk easily on the path created for us, long grass on either side standing tall.

I have come to Kleva to seek the continued aid of the Klevish. They are more than happy to share their technology with humanity, giving us access to the stars, to advanced terraforming techniques, and much more, all at a very reasonable price. But in each negotiation, there is always a demand.

Through some method I do not understand, they choose a Negotiator from among human volunteers who must complete a task to seal the agreement. Our xenosociologists haven't solved the riddle of what, if anything, connects the Negotiators they select, nor the tasks. One negotiation involved playing and winning an elaborate game played with tiny, exquisite moving figures. Another time a Negotiator was tasked with maintaining the health of a pond for a full year. One Negotiator composed poetry.

We have walked for kilometers when Korvach, moving at the same unyielding pace as ever, breaks his silence. He does not take his eyes off the folding path before him.

"Erika-Negotiator, I speak to you now as Korvach-Negotiator, not Korvach-First-Walker. Do you understand?"

"I think so. You now speak not for your religious order, but of our negotiation."

"So it is. I have a task for you. Should you fulfill it, we will share with you the genetic reclamation technology your people request." In typical fashion, he does not say: and if you fail, we will deny it to you. What else should I expect? The Klevish are the most advanced species humanity has encountered, and yet they also prioritize such things as pilgrimage across uninhabited islands and cryptic, puzzling negotiations.

"I understand," I say.

"Your task is to discover why the grass kneels before our passing." He walks on. For the first time in many years I feel a spark of excitement, and the desire to solve a mystery, to learn something new. I am surprised by joy. That joy pulls me forward, and brings with it echoes of the past.

I WAS PACKING for Venus when Maebh poked her head into the bedroom and laughed. I flushed with embarrassment.

"What?" I asked. I was sitting on the bed, surrounded

by stacks of clothing, shoes, research notes, bio-scanners,
transmitters, packing and unpacking them as I tried to
make a year's worth of gear fit into just one suitcase. Maebh
had only a sturdy backpack braced against her shoulders.

"I'm laughing at you, silly," she said so sweetly that I
couldn't hold it against her. "We're not headed to one of
the Far Colonies."

"It's always wise to be prepared," I said, defensively.
"That's one philosophy," she said. "And it's useful when
putting together a research grant. But when it comes to
the actual trip, I prefer a different one." I arched my
eyebrow. "And what's that?"

"Travel light," she said.

I grunted. "Easy for you to say. You're not responsible
for the equipment, the logistics—"

"I know, I know." She sat down next to me, put an arm
around me. For all her talk of travelling lightly, her pack
was heavy enough that the bed sank down where she
sat, pulling everything, including me, toward her. "You
are thorough and rigorous, and I appreciate it. But when
we're dealing with the storms on the equator, you won't
want to be lugging around extra weight."

"I just want the necessary amount of weight," I said,
and offered what I hoped was a playful pout.

"I can help," she promised. "We just focus on what's
essential and leave the rest." Her grin was an admonition
and a tease and a promise all at once.

"Focus on what's essential," I said, cupping her cheek in
my hand. "I like that."

Eventually, we finished packing.

ODIN SENDS HIS ravens out into the world to gather
knowledge, for he is an old god, and wise, and he knows

that he must learn much if he is to prevent Ragnarök. Among the things he knows is that he likely cannot prevent it. The end is coming for him, for all the gods. But he continues to seek a way to change the future. While the birds are flown from him, it as if he is dead or never-born. When they return, his fate is one day nearer.

KORVACH WALKS ON through the bowing grass. I follow along with him as best I can. He never hurries, never shows any sense of urgency. He is implacable. I suspect that he could walk day and night across the entire pilgrimage if he had to do so. He stops promptly at sundown, though, and the pilgrims at the back slump to the ground. I join them, for I am even more exhausted than they are. They have no need to perform tests on the grass, then rush to catch up with him repeatedly as I do. I suspect their sleep is not haunted, as mine has been, with dreams of the past.

My bio-scanner develops analyses of the grass, the soil, the entire biome. It is of little use until I find the right questions to ask, however. Korvach must know this, just as he knows the answer to the riddle he has posed me. And I think he knows I am struggling. On the third day, when I catch up with him again from examining another sample, he does not speak until I catch my breath.

"How is your progress, Erika-Negotiator?" he asks, his stride never slowing.

I reflect on my struggles before answering. "Each day I test hypotheses," I tell him. He tilts his head slightly. I am beginning to recognize the Klevish facial expressions. I think this means the answer suits him.

"If you wish to discuss what you have learned, I will always listen," he says.

Currently my scanner is tracing the product of
microprocessors I injected into a stalk, to see if there is some
subterranean connection between individual plants I haven't
detected. If the signals spread to other plants, I will be close
to an answer. In the meantime, I find myself happy to talk.
"First I checked to see if all the stalks are part of a single
organism, as with some plants on Earth," I told him. "I see,"
he says, inclining his head; he suspected I would try this.

"They are not. Next I checked pheromone signaling."

"And?"

"Nothing I can detect."

"Ah, the smell of the fields," he says. "Each year for
a hundred and fifteen years I have made this journey,
and each year the smell is a connection to my past." The
afternoon is thick with the scent of cut apples and roasted
peppers. It is a smell to hold on to.

"I've never seen anything like it," I say. "There's no
macroscopic fauna I can find on this whole island, and no
other flora, either. Just the grass stretching endless."

The place is impossible to discuss without slipping into
something approaching poetry. As though it is opaque to
science , I think grimly. But the Klevish chose me from
among many volunteers; surely they picked a biologist for
a reason. Perhaps they know of my work with dolphins.

"It is the practice of our faith," he says. Such a strange
way to put it.

"I will run more tests," I say. "If fortune is with me,
each failure will bring me closer to success."

"Each step takes us closer to the coast," he says, and I
wonder if he is chastising me, or urging me on.

A YEAR AFTER we returned from Venus, I came home to find

Maebh staring out over the sea. The view was spectacular, each Manhattan high-rise resting on reclaimed junk turned into a home for coral. Two hundred feet beneath us, life bloomed in the once-dead seas.

She looked out over the water, and for a moment I was completely content. The view was a daily reminder of the work we had done, the painstaking but rewarding process of healing the seas. Each day I taught enthusiastic students at the flotilla, and each night I came home to Maebh. What more could I ask?

That's when I caught sight of her reflection in the glass. Her eyes were red, her cheeks slick. She paced away when I met her gaze, but I hurried to her. "What's wrong?"

"A letter came for you," she said. I rushed to the table. There was only one reason anyone would hire a courier to deliver a physical document. Sure enough, the letter was emblazoned by the seal of the flotilla. I felt Maebh watching me as I broke the seal and read.

When I looked up at her, she had twisted her hands into tight knots, and was working ineffectually to keep her face neutral.

"They've approved it." I fought to keep the excitement out of my voice. "The whole grant." I would be overseeing a team of students working on the next phase, the dolphin reintroduction program. That meant job security and a significant budget and a chance to play a major role in reshaping the whole of the Atlantic.

"Good," she said, and I was shocked to realize she didn't mean it. From the look on her face, she was, too. "I mean, I'm glad for you, Erika. I know how hard you've been working for it."

"We've been working for it," I say. Outside the sunset cast the sea in pink and gold.

She gave me a look that shatters me each time I think about it. "Anyway," she said, "Congratulations."

"What is this? I thought you'd be happy for me."

She hesitated. "I thought so too. I told myself I'd be happy for you. For us. But sometimes—sometimes the world doesn't unfold the way we hope."

I could feel my jaw hanging open. I forced it closed. "This is the opportunity of a lifetime."

"Yes," she said. "And it will be your life. It will open project after project to you. They'd be a fool to let you get away."

"What's wrong with that?" I felt anger bubbling up, anger I didn't understand.

"It's the endpoint," she said, and paced over to the window. The city's lights were burning against the last of the day. "It means you'll never take a field assignment on Europa or a colony or..."

"We could never hope to get an appointment this good off world."

"Probably not," she said, and was silent so long I was surprised when she continued. "Do you remember that night on Venus when we watched the *Erinaceus venaeus* foraging?"

We'd watched it for close to an hour, its small nose exploring the undergrowth, rooting through the rich loam, looking so much like its cousins on earth, save that it was slightly smaller and its coat was a shimmering green.

"I could never forget it. It's the most beautiful thing I've ever seen." I said.

"You told me then that you never wanted to stop exploring."

Oh. "I—this is a kind of exploring. Rebuilding what we've lost."

She ran a hand through her hair and turned back to me. "Earth's going to be okay," she said. "Even if you didn't take the grant, someone else would get it and reintroduce the dolphins. Why does it have to be you?"

"Because I'm good at it, Maebh, and because it's worth doing."

"Yes," she said. "And it means we're staying here forever, rebuilding what we've previously fucked up, when there's everything out there."

I was still clutching the delicate acceptance letter. My hands shook. I could see the shape things were taking, and I felt something awful curl itself within me.

WHEN HUGINN RETURNS and Muninn is absent, Odin is lost. His mind is alive with Thought, but with no Memory to guide him, he cannot plan for Ragnarök. He cannot draw on the wisdom of the past. He is useless, incapable of action, for his mind is as blank as and shapeless as a block of stone.

ON THE FIFTH night, the pilgrims camp just beyond a rise. While they settle in, I backtrack and sit on the bare rock at its peak. I watch the sky as the stars come out in their unfamiliar constellations. This is my first trip outside of the Sol system. For a long time I had no wish for such a trip, until restlessness or regret changed my mind.

The night here is darker than any on earth, with no moon, nothing but the stars and the rustling of the grass. It is a beauty as vibrant as any field of flowers, yet somehow as desolate as a desert.

I do not notice Korvach has come up behind me until he speaks.

"Is it a sight worth seeing?"

"Very much so," I say. "I wish—there is someone I very much wish could see it." Maebh would have loved it here. But if she were still with me, I would never have followed this path. Korvach is comfortable with silence. He does not press me, but neither does he hurry on.

Finally I speak again. "There is no trace of a neural network, and no microfauna that would explain the grass's behavior." A team of experts with proper equipment would no doubt crack the case quickly. But whatever the Klevish want me to learn, I alone must discover it.

"I am told," Korvach says, and sits beside me, "that on Earth many people practice a meditation of stillness."

"It's true," I say. "More than one of our faiths teach such things." I do not see the connection, but it is a better topic than my failure to find answers.

"You would commune with me, Erika-Negotiator, if you would share whether you keep such a faith."

"I do not keep them. Once I thought I could never be still, and then the time for movement had passed before I realized I had already halted."

"A sad thing," he said. "I too could not keep a faith of stillness. I must keep moving forward, for movement is life. And how else will the Path know us?"

"I thought 'Known Path' referred to you knowing the path."

"One could not be true without the other," he says, and stands. "Good night, Erika-Negotiator. We resume our journey at dawn." It is a reminder of how little time I have left. In less than a day, the pilgrimage will be over, and I will have succeeded or failed.

I stay some time on the rise and then push my way toward camp through the grass: it has already risen behind us. When sleep takes me, I dream of Maebh, and of Ravens.

§

I DID NOT need to check the time to know that Maebh's ship would be leaving soon. Beneath me, the Earth spread like a familiar face. Each year she grew more beautiful, each year a bit more green. In my lifetime she would be as green as in the old images. And long after I am dead, perhaps Maebh will look down on a world so verdant one would not know it was the work of many generations to salvage it.

I turned away from the viewport to find Maebh watching me. For once, she stood still, her backpack thrown over her shoulder. The strap was ragged around the edges, and the seams were caked with dirt.

"The Captain wants me on board in five," she said. Her eyes shone, though with sadness or excitement I couldn't say. On impulse, I took her hands. The last moments, the last of us, and I couldn't find anything to say.

"It's not too late, you know," she said. "You can still come with us." The colony ship would take a qualified biologist in a moment. They'd take almost anyone who was willing to head four hundred years to the ragged edge of human exploration. "Or you could stay." I expected anger, I think. I was so miserable I would have picked a fight just to be sure she felt something. But she looked at me with pity.

"There's a whole universe out there, worlds where humans have never set foot. I can't turn my back on that."

"But you can turn your back on me?"

That did it. "After all this, I thought you'd want me to be happy."

"I want us to be happy." Behind her was the embrace of the Milky Way and a moon-bright lance—a vessel accelerating toward relativistic speeds.

"We don't want the same things anymore," she said, as though I didn't know it keenly.

"You could be happy with me," I insisted. "You don't have to throw away everything we've built together."

"I'm not throwing it away, Erika. The past is always there. It's a tool for discovering the future." It took me a very long time to make sense of that. "I have to go," she continued after a moment.

We kissed, and she turned away.

When she was almost gone down the corridor, I shouted after her. "Will you think of me?" She glanced over her shoulder, flashed a smile. "You'll always be part of me." Then she turned the corner. I wasn't right for a long time after that.

◊

HUGINN DOES NOT return, but Muninn does. Odin's consciousness has fled, but guided by memory, he follows the path laid out for him. Each step enacts the promise of the one before, and each enables the next. Thus he faces the future.

◊

AHEAD OF THE pilgrims, a single point of light: a ship in the bay, ready to collect us and take us to civilization. I rush through the high grass, holding the sensor high above my head. I find Korvach keeping his steady pace. We will reach the bay hours from now, as the sun dips behind the waves.

"Korvach," I shout, then hold my side as I try to catch my breath. He does not slow.

"Yes?" His tone is serene, but his face tilts in what might be a smile.

"When you take this pilgrimage—do you set out and finish at the same time each year?"

"We do." Definitely a smile.

"Down to the minute, I believe."

"Yes, Erika-Negotiator, we do. Why do you ask?"

"Because I think I've solved it."

"And what have you discovered?"

"It's prions."

He does not stop, but he shifts his whole torso to face me as he walks, reminding me of a curious corvid. I push on.

"Prion folding, specifically. Proteins that pass on their shape to other nearby proteins. In fauna, prions can be deadly—misfolding proteins in the brain, for example. It creates a cascade. A similar process in plants on Earth can allow them to react to changes in their environment. But nothing on earth rises to the level of information retention in your grass."

"I see." Of course he knew all this already; the test was to demonstrate what I had learned.

"The prions solve the problem that the plants don't have brains or nervous system. They don't need them— they don't need to interpret, to understand. The prions function as their memory, so they react based on past stimulus. They don't think, but they remember.

"It is as you say, Erika-Negotiator," Korvach says. "May I ask how you arrived at this insight?"

"I've been thinking," I say, "of stories my mother taught me. And of words–words of wisdom from someone I love. About the use of memory. And then I realized plants could have a kind of memory, too."

"Your insight communes with the grass, and with me," Korvach says.

We walk on together for some time, toward the beach. I have been lost for so long. It feels good to know where I am heading. The stars come out one by one.

"I think I would like to know more of your faith, Korvach," I say.

He tilts his face up to the sky in a gesture I have never seen. "I very much hoped you would, Erika-Pilgrim. Let us walk together."

The grass communes with us by bowing down; we commune with it by following its path into the future, by moving forward.

Five Reasons
for the Sign Above
Her Door,
One of Them
Unspoken

L ILITH HAS KEPT her eye on the young man for two days, since he arrived at her hostel. Why was he there? Was he like her, like most of her guests? He showed no outward signs, but that meant nothing: he might have been hiding his nature to make the road a bit safer, or (though it pained her to consider) someone might have altered him, stripped away all external signs. But his eyes told a different story, a desire that was not for community, not for hope. A voyeur's gaze.

Once she knew what he was, she invited him into her office, where the sign above the door held the old notation from maps, marking the border of the known: *here there be monsters.*

And when she set him down, she told him nothing but the truth. But there are truths she does not tell him.

§

1. THE FIRST TRUTH answers his too-eager gaze: I am real. The fox-fur on her limbs, not as soft as it had once

been, ragged in places from cuts and burns, but still lovely enough to turn heads. The goat-eyes always watching him. She is what he came to see.

"I am real," she tells him. "Here, in my office, you may stare." He does not seem to notice the implied ban.

2. WHEN SHE CAN see he is going to start talking, she tells him another truth. The truth about her adolescence, when her fur curled from her skin and her eyes changed, the pupil reforming, the blue turning to gold. How her parents forced her to shave daily, to wear shades, and when the growth came too fast even for daily shaving, how they tried other methods. "Anti-divergence therapies," as the doctors called them, did nothing for the changes, but nevertheless made Lilith vomit, and when there was nothing else in her stomach, she would wretch bile.

"They found another doctor," she tells the young man. "Who would prescribe experimental radiation therapy. The risk, you see, was worth it. For them. They wanted to fix me."

The young man shifts in his seat uncomfortably. The fact that he can be unsettled is a good sign.

3. SHE TELLS HIM that, rather than face the radiation, she ran away, wearing long sleeves and gloves even in the worst of the summer. At first she was terrified of being found, being returned, but as she traveled, she realized there was a greater danger: men who sought out Chimeric hitchhikers for their own ends. Some were mere fetishists, too invasive in their questions, their glances, but nothing more. Others would take what they wished, and sometimes they would leave bodies behind, after.

In fear of these horrors, Lilith met others like her, other Chimera, on the run, whispering to one another, sometimes banding together, trying to stay alive.

"Today they say my generation was the first," she tells him. "But that isn't right. We are just the first they acknowledged."

She thinks often of the horrors of the past, before Chimeras came together for aid and protection, when their very existence was hushed up by families, or worse. She does not know if she can make this young man understand, but she has decided to give him a chance, to answer his curiosity with knowledge.

His eyes move restlessly over her body as she speaks.

4. SHE SPEAKS OF the night she nearly froze to death. She'd been traveling with three others, Colt (ze had a Texas drawl, a slow smile, and a sharp knife ready to answer any danger), Danny (who had lost an arm to a "treatment," and who was the kindest boy she'd ever met), and a gray-eyed girl who spoke in sign-language and never gave her name. The late-spring blizzard caught them unprepared. They huddled together under an overpass as temperatures plummeted, snow and ice blowing horizontally, their clothing soaking through.

"There was nowhere we could go," she tells him. "We were safer with the storm than with strangers, you see. All we had was each other."

He is listening now, his jaw set with tension. She sees the empathy in his eyes. Perhaps he too has known skin-flaying cold, or some other bone-deep pain.

She cannot hope to convey to him the horror of that night, the burning cold that infected her dreams, dreams indistinguishable from reality. All through the night they had only flimsy cardboard shelter and each other.

The terror and wonder of having nothing but body-heat to offer, and to give freely from that meager supply.

There are no words, so she shows him her left hand, the stubs that had been her fourth and fifth fingers, welcomes his gaze.

"Sometime that night," she tells him, "I promised myself that I would survive, and that I'd make a place so people like me could always find shelter if they needed it. The storm nearly took everything from me. But it gave me the dream of this hostel."

5. WHEN HE LEAVES her office, she does not know if he will learn to be something more than a voyeur. She doesn't know if he will ever see her fellow Chimera as fully human. But she knows that he will not harm them.

She smiles, for she is somewhat fond of him, likes him despite herself, likes him because she has a fondness for travelers and hope for the future.

There is another reason for her smile, a truth she shares with no one. Twice, men have come to her hostel who meant danger. They brought knives and ropes and starving eyes, and they thought to find vulnerable targets. People no one would miss, they thought.

Her smile is because this young man is no threat, and so will not join them, lye-packed and buried deep.

Here there be monsters, the sign reads: a welcome for some, for others a warning.

Everything
the Sea Takes,
It Returns

EVERYTHING THE SEA takes, it gives back in its own way and its own time. That was what Jess's grandmother believed, what she'd told Jess as they stood in the shadow of the giant red cedar that had washed ashore, its severed roots thicker than Jess's body. It must have drifted for a thousand years or more to return to them in that moment.

So, when the virus takes Jess's grandmother, Jess steers her little solar-powered boat out past the channel islands and gives the body to the sea. She is sixteen, old enough to know the sea's ways, that if her grandmother returned, it would be through the cycles of life. She'd be part of the food chain, better at least than plastic and algal blooms. Sixteen, and old enough to know the truth, but young enough to fantasize that the beloved woman would come striding up the beach, her skin kelp-green, her hair flowing along unseen currents.

AT TWENTY, JESS finds the waterlogged duffle bag, its nylon

handles tangled in a cluster of driftwood. The plastic bags inside are sealed, and the powder they protected is untouched. She feels her stomach turn, wonders in what manner the sea took this, and why it has returned it here, returned it to her and Lana.

"What if someone comes looking for it?" she asks, though it had clearly been in the water for a long time, because she can't name her true fear.

"The sea gave it to us," Lana says, and Jess can't deny this. "It means for us to have it."

Jess thinks the sea's reasons are more opaque, that gods act in their own ways and for their own reasons. But the shelter they're living in is run by a fundamentalist group, and they can't even share a bed. So they do what Lana says they must, and for the first time in years, things are truly good. For a while.

MILITIAS FROM THE other side of the mountains push towards the coast, and soon it might not be safe for two girls to be together. Worse, the militias are eliminating the competition. Lana, cunning, tough, fearless, insists these are solvable problems, though Jess wants only to run.

"What makes you think it's safer anywhere else?" Lana asks.

Since Jess couldn't abide the thought of leaving the sea, of abandoning Lana, she stays.

They last longer than anyone would have expected. But they can't fix the world.

FOR YEARS AFTER she loses Lana, every time Jess wanders the beach she dreads what the sea might return to her:

Lana's heavily-Sharpied sneakers, a rotting foot still inside;
great clots of plastic waste, death given form; the necklace
Jess had saved for and proudly given Lana when they were
young and couldn't have imagined that anyone could hate
them enough to give Lana to sea.

Her dreams are sea-haunted, thick with briny toxins
and the dead with eyes like dark candles. After each
dream, she swears she's done with the sea, meaning to
turn inland at last, stop her aimless migration up and
down the coastline, trying to stay ahead of the militia, but
not trying as hard as she should have. It was Lana they'd
wanted most of all, but they'll kill Jess too, if they get the
chance. She half wishes for that, her body weary, her face
battered by sun and saltwind, by grief. She never does
make it far from the sea.

Just as no coastline is impervious, just as the sea claims what
it will, grief can hollow a heart. Who can say what will fill it?

The woman walks along the surf. Jess watches her,
wary. The stranger kneels, scoops water into a vial, caps
it, and moves on. At times she stops to gather refuse from
the beach and stuffs it into a bag at her hip. Jess does not
understand, but sees a pattern, evidence of a purpose, and
that's enough.

Eventually the woman stops, sits on a rock above the
high tide line. Jess approaches. The woman looks up with
neither surprise nor malice.

"I wondered if you were going to keep following me
forever," she says. Jess imagines what it would be like to be
so unafraid.

"What are you doing?" she asks.

"Collecting samples," the woman says, and gestures
for Jess to sit. She does, and the woman shares her bread.

Not rations, or even grain packed with wood fibers, but real bread. They eat in silence, and Jess feels the dull ache in her gut flare to a fire, the hunger becoming more intense by being partially sated.

They gather every last crumb. "That's all the food I have," the woman tells Jess. "But if you'd keep me company, I'll show you what I'm doing."

Jess has nothing better to do, and there might be more food, no matter what the woman says. They tread the beach, taking samples at regular intervals. To heal the ocean, the woman explains, to make it again fit for life.

"There's no fixing it," Jess says, her voice frail and bitter in the cold wind. "We're less than plankton to it. How could you even hope to fix something so massive?" She hates herself for the question, for the desperation she hears in it.

"Healing, not fixing," the woman insists. "And I can't. Not on my own. This is the work of thousands of people, on many shores. We're gathering data, and computers are using it to run simulations—"

"There aren't any computers left."

"There are." The woman stoops to gather a sample, holds the vial up to Jess, who seals it in the way she's been shown. "Powered by solar farms or the heat beneath the earth. And there are still radios to call in data, even over oceans."

They walk in silence.

"Everything is shattered," Jess says. "The ocean most of all." Farther down, the waves bloom green with algae, the only life that could thrive in its heat-scorched, plastic-swamped depths.

The woman looks at her sadly, a look so near to pity that Jess bristles. "Maybe," the woman concedes. "But it still feels good to do the work."

◊

THE WOMAN'S NAME is Cyn. Not short for Cynthia, she tells Jess. Nor short for anything. She camps near the beach, and they share body heat. Jess stays with her, heating rations, digging latrines, recording data, anything to earn her keep, though Cyn hasn't asked her to. Jess does not want to be indebted. They speak little. Days turn to weeks.

"It's good that you're learning this," Cyn says one night after they've run their simple tests, radioed in their results.

"Why good?" Jess asks, fearing a trap, a complication.

"If something happens to me, you'll know how to carry on. How to report from these shores."

Who says I'll carry on without you? Jess almost says, but stops herself. It is better to wander with a task than without.

"Nothing will happen to you," her voice is flat, the lie thick on her lips.

Cyn holds her gaze for a long moment, then turns back to the sea. "We both know no one can be sure of that." Though they never speak of their griefs, the world is full of them, the shoreline a catalog of all that has been lost.

"Then why go on?" Jess asks, minutes later. "Why fight against it?" She doesn't know what she meant by "it."

Cyn shrugs. "Why do you go on?" A scar a half-inch thick runs along her neck. During the day she wears high collars, but in the tent at night Jess has seen it circling her neck, angry, puckered white-pink.

Jess has no answer.

§

THEIR PACE IS deliberate, but every coast yields to time. The years lap like waves. They work for food and supplies when they must, take gifts when they're offered, which happens with a frequency that never ceases to surprise Jess.

"People want to help each other," Cyn says. "Most people. More than you give them credit for."

They're sometimes threatened, cursed, attacked. One man, blank-eyed and wire-strong, shares a meal with them, then attacks Cyn. Jess is prepared and does what's necessary.

"I wish you weren't so trusting," Jess says after they give his body to the sea.

"I've spent too much time being afraid," Cyn says. "I'm done with it."

THEIR SILENCES GROW more comfortable, then begin to crack. Jess tells Cyn of her grandmother, about the homeless shelters, about what the sea smelled like when she was young. She never speaks of Lana.

She keeps an inventory of things she has learned about Cyn: when she was born, people called her a boy, and kept saying that until she told them no, she wasn't, and then even after that; the scar on her neck was given to her, but the ones on her wrists, bone-white and fine as needles, she gave to herself; she had a brother, once; she can imitate the sounds of seabirds that Jess has not heard in many years, but cannot carry a tune; she is often in pain, though she never speaks of it; her eyes are blue, but when she has been crying they look green, flecked with glints of gold shine.

Which is to say that Jess is in love with Cyn, even though she tried not to be, even though love is a kind of debt. Nothing physical is between them, nothing besides the sharing of body heat on cold nights, but Jess believes Cyn loves her too, though she doubts Cyn is in love with her.

And one more fact: Cyn is dying. The realization comes slowly but Jess can't deny it. Cyn's body slowly consumes itself, her hands cold, her steps slower. One day Jess will give her to the sea, and then—

She doesn't know. Her own personal extinction event is coming, and she cannot imagine anything after it.

§

JESS'S GRANDMOTHER RETURNS to her dreams, her skull like bleached coral; her limbs a tangle of seaweed, her mouth lolling open. Jess wakes with a scream stillborn on her lips.

§

THEY SIT ON a rocky outcropping. There was a pier here, once. Its remaining pillars slice like canines from the waves. The sea is golden in the late afternoon sun. Far out, visible only as a dark line on the horizon, is a living mat. Ruslav and Iona, speaking to them over the radio, have told them of the biological lattice on which the mat grows. Musa described the bacteria that consume plastic, the great vines of seaweed snaking down into the depths, which may someday play a small role in food-chain restoration efforts. Jess and Cyn understand only a small portion of this project, as do all the others. Perhaps the AIs that coordinate understand more, but there is no one in charge, no one vantage from which all becomes clear. A million interlocking labors, an ecosystem of harm mitigation.

"It's beautiful," Jess says. "I never really thought I'd see it."

"So many ways it can go wrong," Cyn replies. Alarm surges through Jess. This sounds like despair, something she'd never expected from Cyn. She doesn't look at her friend, chooses her words with care.

"Yes," she says. "Many ways. But still worth trying."

The sun arcs towards night. Each wave is a light-tipped flash over dark water.

"I thought that would be enough," Cyn's voice sounds far away. "But one comes to the end and wonders...what I mean is, I'm wondering what it was all for."

Jess has wondered this many times, but had never thought to hear it from Cyn's lips. She doesn't have an answer, only a story. So she tells her of Lana, that name breaking through a dam of silence, and how they were clever and in love and thought they could do anything. And how it had ended in the only way it could.

"Oh, Jess, I'm so sorry," Cyn says, and Jess doesn't know how to make herself understood, how to say what's held her together in the years since they took Lana from her.

Night creeps over the beach. The stars blossom like they never did in Jess's childhood, not even far out from the city. A dead satellite streaks overhead.

"I'd hoped I'd see results in my lifetime," Cyn says. "For a happier ending."

"This is my happier ending," Jess says, and knows it is true, even though Lana deserved to share it with her, even though it may be a kind of betrayal to admit it.

"Is this all life is? Is our destiny to try and build something and watch it all wash away?" Cyn leans on her shoulder, one arm around her. She has faded away of late, is becoming insubstantial. But for now she is here.

"I don't believe in destiny." Jess wipes at her eyes. "Maybe we just didn't understand the systems that we were caught in. Like tourists—when I was young, there were still tourists, and if they didn't respect the currents, they'd disappear just like that. They thought because they could swim..."

"I'm sorry," Cyn says. "None of it is fair."

"We thought we were alone." Jess pulls Cyn tighter to her, sharing warmth, because soon they will need to retreat to the tent, and there aren't many days left for them. "I wish Lana and I had known something like this project...I wish we'd found..."

"Community," Cyn says.

"Yes. I wish...oh, Cyn, I wish I could tell you it will all work. That the ocean will thrive again. Oh, I wish you'd let me lie...but this isn't just about the project. I don't think we're growing rafts. I think we're growing a model for a different kind of world."

"I like that," Cyn says, and Jess can hear the smile on her lips.

"I'd hope so." Jess squeezes her shoulder. "You're the one who taught it to me."

The cold soon chases them into the tent, and they share what they have: food, body heat, tenderness.

THERE COMES A morning where Cyn doesn't wake up. Jess washes her body, gives it to the sea. She takes the day's samples, cries until she's empty of tears. When the sun sets, she takes up the radio, and shares the news. None of them are anything but voices to her, just as she and Cyn are—were—voices to them. But they share their grief, their data, their knowledge, their mingled hopes.

JESS FEELS THREE presences with her as she walks the tideline day after day. Or perhaps three absences, like the places the sea has swallowed, now remembered only by rusted road-signs pointing the way to nowhere. The three women in her life, each beloved in different ways. Each given to the sea, each returning only in dreams.

The work sustains Jess, gives her a reason to keep walking. Alone with her ghosts, she sometimes fantasizes about joining them in the depths. But there is Cyn's task to carry on, and the voices sharing themselves across the night, and so she continues her pilgrimage.

One day, she senses she is being followed. A figure not much larger than a child, wary but fascinated. She keeps at her work.

On the third day, as she eats her lunch, the figure approaches. They're young and malnourished, a familiar void in their eyes. Jess shares her small meal with them.

"I don't have anything else to offer," she says, "but if you'd like to help me, I could use the company."

A few days later, she bends to pick up a clump of garbage, but her companion is faster. They hand it to her, but it isn't garbage at all: it's a tangle of hair. No, it's a clump of seaweed, dark green and smelling of her childhood.

Everything we give to the sea comes back to us, Jess knows, though rarely in the ways we expect, the ways we dream.

Shadows of
the Hungry
the Broken,
the Transformed

•—‖—◆❯◆❮◆—‖—•

JUSTINE'S SHADOW WATCHES her. It stands under the
lamp post across from her flat, her smoky
semblance, flickering and shifting under the gaslight.
She's at her window, tea cooling in her hands.
Though the shadow has no eyes, Justine is certain that
it stares at her, just as she is certain it is hers. She would
know it anywhere.

When she finally turns from the window to dump her
cold tea into the sink, she looks down out of old habit, as
though she'll find her shadow once again attached. As
though what has been torn apart could ever be reassembled.

Four months now since she lost her shadow. How many
nights has it been out there, waiting for her, keeping vigil?
And what does it want? She picks up a book, Faulen's *On
the Joyous Uselessness of Heartweaving: A Reflection on Craft
and Purpose*, and flips a few pages before she admits she's
absorbing nothing, sets it aside.

She could confront her shadow, ask what it wants.
Demand it go away. Beg, threaten. To what end? She doesn't
know. It is still there when she closes the drapes. She lies
sleepless on the sofa, unable to face the vastness of her bed.

When Justine steps onto the street the next morning, she's met with the smell of smoke, of ash. The food riots must have resumed, though the Watch had just last week assured the university they had everything under control. Whenever she thinks of the riots, the agony of grief washes over her anew, and it is all she can do to push those thoughts away, unable to bear them.

It's an uncharacteristically sunny day for autumn, with shadows everywhere, thrown by the old stone buildings in the student district, the stately ivy-lined walls of the university, the trees shedding leaves, even the undergraduates going about their days, their shadows trailing from them as though it were the most natural thing in the world. She keeps looking behind her, half-expecting to see her shadow following her, but there is no sign of it.

She has a meeting with Professor Morinth, one she has been putting off until sensing she could no longer reschedule it. She must face him.

"I have sympathy for your situation," Morinth tells her, sitting behind his oiled oak desk, "but there are deadlines to consider." The youngest member of the department of visual art, his face is unlined under a thin beard that does little to make him look older. He won't look directly at her, as though losing one's shadow is catching. At least he still speaks to her. When strangers notice her lack, they either force smiles through gritted teeth or ignore her entirely.

She knows what he's going to say before he says it. She must make progress if she wishes to remain a part of the program. The small stipend she receives is dependent upon that progress. But the work won't come. She lacks the focus even to read, can't handle the analytical side at which she's always excelled, much less the practicum, the heartweaving itself, which is to be the core of her dissertation.

"I will have work to show you, Professor," she says, her own voice sounding distant to her. It seems for a moment she is looking over her own shoulder, observing herself from a distance, though there is no such vantage point in this cramped office. "Soon."

Morinth doesn't believe her and she can't blame him. She's only telling him what she's expected to. There's no conviction in her voice, nor panic, nor even pain. Beaten flat. Not even the knowledge that, without her stipend, the funds she inherited from her mother won't last long.

"See that you do," Morinth says. She is almost at the door when he speaks again. "Ms. Revel." He still won't look at her. "I will not be able to hold a loom for you forever."

There it is, her years of studies nearing an ignominious end. No degree, no more heartweaving. Nothing. She feels as if she should cry, as if another person who finds herself in such a position *would* cry. She leaves his office without a word.

Doctoral Candidates in Heartweaving are allotted one of the tertiary looms. Only those craftspeople who have attained the rank of Doctor of the Holy Arts and maintained an official relationship with the university have use of the Grand Loom. For years, Justine has dreamed of someday working with it, will never forget the first time she saw it, large as a room, its brass filigree almost glowing against the dim, recessed lighting that allowed the threads' own light to illuminate the project. She'd lain awake nights planning what she could accomplish on a machine like that, one capable of working with the finest threads of one's essence. She'd been so sure, then, of her talent, the trajectory of her career.

And Zara had been her eager audience through it all, her belief in Justine's greatness outstripping even the artist's own. Even at their lowest, when Justine had let herself fall back into an ex's destructive orbit and Zara had nearly left her, that faith in Justine's skill had never wavered.

And now Zara was gone. Just a few wrong steps, a moment's inattention on an errand, and she'd been caught between the Watch and the food rioters. And that had been that.

The tertiary looms are much less impressive than the Grand Loom, but even so they are valuable beyond words, for only at such a true heartloom can one weave from their own essence. Perhaps a handful are in private ownership, and rumors place one at the Lord Mayor's residence. Aside from those, there are no heartlooms in the city but those at the university. Standing before her assigned loom, its functional but uninspiring lines taking almost every available inch of space in the cramped studio, Justine can't imagine how she ever had the confidence to use it, the control and technique to draw from herself what was needed, to pull threads from her mind as easily as singers draw melodies from their lungs. She prepares the loom with what remains of the thread she pulled from herself when Zara was still alive. A simple pattern, one she's long used as an exercise.

Traditional weaving requires precision and planning, intricately preparing the warp in advance. Heartweaving, pulling as it does from oneself, is a very different skill. It allows one to create the warp's essence as one works, allowing for greater control and improvisation, while also requiring great focus and precision. Such is the price of creating a weave out of nothing but oneself. Or perhaps the heartloom's function is very different. Some theorists claim it simply holds space onto which the True Warp is created.

There are many debates about heartweaving, including over the best way to induce the desired threads to emerge, but Justine has never found a better technique than to weave a pattern that's as easy to her as breathing, pulling in more complex elements as threads emerge from her chest as they sprout like spring flowers, which are then guided by the arcane harness down her arms and then fed into the loom that incorporates them into the warp.

Her hands and feet move on without the need for thought. The threads are thin as spiderweb, reds and purples, blues so dark they are almost black, bluewhites like lightning that hurt to stare at directly, ochre and pearl and a green like the last flash of daylight, all laid down in a geometric pattern, one of the first she mastered, its shape and rules better known to her than her own body. A weave she can produce without thought, an elegant expression of the perfect, glorious uselessness of her art, conveying no meaning, only beauty, a pattern she can weave without the constant need to intellectualize, to explain, to develop grand theories about how to produce from her own essence the colors and textures of thread she seeks.

But the thread she has on hand runs low, and no more emerges from within her. The loom whirs on with the comforting sounds of the thread unspooling, the shuttles passing through the shed. The pattern unfolds itself as though she is unnecessary to the process, but the spools waiting to be filled with her essence remain empty. The weave comes to a stop, half-finished, its resources depleted, its creator barren.

JUSTINE DOESN'T NOTICE the stranger approach. No surprise, since she sits with her head in her hands, staring

at the manicured lawn, shining green under the sunlight.
In mid-afternoon, the quad is too busy, and she's not
ready to return to her empty flat. She's chosen instead the
stillness of the grounds around the reflecting pool, which
are rarely crowded, and even when others are present
their voices don't rise above whispers.

A gentle cough startles her. Above her stands a
young woman, wearing the unadorned robes of an
undergraduate. It is a minor violation of etiquette for her
to approach a doctoral candidate unbidden, but Justine
has no use for such rules.

"Can I help you?" Justine whispers.

The woman pulls a thread of red hair from a freckle-
dusted face. "I hope we can help each other," she says
and glances around, as if worried she will be sanctioned
for disturbing Justine's stillness. She holds out a sliver of
paper, which Justine studies for a moment, then takes from
her. She expects the woman to say something, to clarify,
or perhaps even to apologize. But the undergraduate just
nods and walks away without looking back.

When she is out of sight, Justine unfolds the paper.

Facing It Together, the paper reads, along with an address
on the edge of the student district, near the mills. *Every
Thirdday evening, seven bells.*

It makes no sense. It is as if she's been invited to a secret
society in the most awkward possible way. And there is
something else, something wrong with interaction, that
she struggles to identify.

She retreats to the library, unwilling to walk home
while the sun sinks low in the sky, and only then does she
realize why she hadn't noticed the woman's approach: she
too had cast no shadow.

&

JUSTINE WAITS FOR full dark to return home, looking through the library's stacks for information on detached shadows, but there is next to nothing. Unsurprising. Those with shadows typically want nothing to do with those whose have been severed, and what shadowless person would wish to draw attention to their condition, to lay open their wound for all to see? The thought is stomach-turning. Horrific.

When she heads back to her flat, night's veil is drawn over the world, and she can almost forget about shadows. Until each pool of lamplight reminds her, every bench and garbage bin throwing their own darkness, until Justine feels as though she's a soap bubble about to pop.

The night is unnaturally still. The Watch have announced another round of curfews. It hurts too much to focus on such things, and she has no need to. She has special dispensation, documents from the university that state she is a doctoral candidate and so allowed to be on the street after curfew, such is the university's clout and wealth. Even so, most candidates won't venture out after dark. The consensus is that it is safer that way.

Not safe enough. Zara bled out on the pavement in broad daylight, as did the others who had been felled by the barrage of musket fire.

Lost in those thoughts, she has almost forgotten about what awaits her until she turns the corner onto her block, and there it stands, a dark translucence in the light. No eyes, no mouth, nothing but the outline of Justine, yet she is certain it sensed her coming, has turned its full attention to her.

She reaches the doorway to her building, fumbles with the keys. It is coming for her. She can sense it, its weightless bulk closing on her until—

And then she is inside. She slams the heavy door, the building's foyer echoing with its sound. She can't resist looking through the peephole. Her shadow stands where she left it, waiting.

Later, awake on the couch, in the unnatural stillness of the curfew-silenced night, she wonders if it will ever stop waiting, and if she will ever be able to weave again. And then a terrible thought: is it even possible to heartweave without one's shadow? No one has told her otherwise, but then, who would?

In her grief after Zara's death, she lost her shadow. If she has lost her craft, too, there is nothing left.

§

WHATEVER JUSTINE EXPECTED from 'Facing It Together,' it was not this vast, low-ceilinged cellar with dirt floors and rock walls. People sit in a circle in the center of the room. She knows none of their names, though she recognizes the freckled woman and one or two others, perhaps from passing them on the street, sharing a classroom with them, or some other tenuous connection.

The room is clearly used for storage most of the time, with sagging boxes and haphazardly stacked clutter making vague outlines against the dark walls. Around the gathered group, braziers burn, a dozen of them, their flame-light directed inward by curving brass backdrops. The room is dark, but the circle is bright as day. Brighter. Taking her position amidst the others, Justine sees the reason for the arrangement: with so many light sources, there are no true shadows. No temptation to see if everyone here was truly shadowless, or if some merely have wounded shadows or are con artists.

Justine half expects a con. Why else would the shadowless gather? Why would anyone volunteer their own incompleteness? It feels like picking at a scab, only much worse. Why, then, is she here? *Because it is something other than being home*, she tells herself, but knows that is not the full truth.

There are eight of them in the circle, the youngest an
adolescent still in their school clothes, the oldest a man
whose weather-beaten face looks as ancient and hostile as
a blighted mountainside. Some are students, a couple have
the calloused hands and hungry frames of millworkers.
One bears herself like an aristocrat, and the silk clothes
she wears suggest it is no affectation.

"We are gathered to create a space of honesty and
mutual support." Justine notices the silence only when
words break it. The speaker is one of the mill workers,
maybe a decade older than Justine. "Even when those
goals are in tension, we must honor both of them as best
we can." There are nods from the group, murmurs of
agreement. Justine suspects she is the only newcomer.

"All are welcome to share or stay silent, as they wish,"
the woman says. She does not give her name, nor do any
of the others who speak after her.

"In my dreams, my shadow is still attached," a young
man in student robes says. "I used to have dreams where
I was falling or flying. Now I have just this one. It's sunset.
I'm walking down a quiet lane. I look back, and there it is."

A murmur of sympathy, then a silence. "Would you
share with us how the dreams make you feel?" the
woman asks. Justine sees her as their de facto leader. She
is younger than Justine had first thought, but her back is
bent, her forehead creased with worry.

"Joyous," the man says. "Like I was whole again. And
then I wake up, it hits me all over again."

"If we aren't what we once were, that doesn't mean we
aren't whole," Freckles says, and Justine feels a tension in
the room, a site of dispute.

The sharing moves on slowly. At first it seems others
are reluctant to speak, but it isn't that. They carefully wait
until whoever is speaking has truly finished, and Justine is
certain some of them won't utter a word until they figure
out exactly what they wish to say.

There is something perverse in hearing others talk
about their missing shadows. One of Justine's earliest
memories is of playing with another child on a stoop.
As it grew dark, she realized the other child didn't have
a shadow. She asked about it with the directness of
childhood, and her mother immediately apologized to
the other girl and pulled Justine away. *We don't ask such
questions*, her mother said, and would say no more.

As an adolescent she'd heard people whispering about
it, snickering behind the backs of fellow students unlucky
enough to have parents without shadows, and she even
joined in occasionally, the breaking of the taboo the point
in itself. Everyone knows about the shadowless, but most
have the good grace not to speak of it.

This, though—it makes her skin crawl. When someone
speaks, all eyes turn toward them. Everyone knows what
sort of things happen to someone to strip them of their
shadow, that only the worst emotional wounds can cause
it. To be known for it, to have everyone wondering about
the source, certain only that it was terrible—

Justine realizes she is shaking. She pulls her legs up
under her chin, grits her teeth. No, no, this is the last
thing she needs. The others' voices are far away as if they
echo from far down a tunnel.

"...I just want to know it is okay," someone says. "The
thought of it out there, alone, hurting..."

Justine climbs to her feet, her body like a distant
automaton, out of her control. "I'm sorry," she hears herself
stammer, and then she is up the cellar stairs, on her knees,
emptying her stomach onto the alleyway. She retches
long after there is anything to lose, and only then does she
realize someone is holding her hair back from her face.

Justine wipes her lips on the back of her hand and turns to
see Freckles crouching beside her, her face pinched with worry.

"Are you all right?" she asks, one arm around Justine as
though she might collapse, even though the weaver is on

her knees and has one hand bracing herself, even though there isn't much further to fall.

"Yes," Justine manages. "I just needed air..."

"Let me help you home."

"No, I can..." Justine doesn't finish the sentence. The struggle to get to her feet requires intense focus. When she finally manages it, she realizes the other woman is supporting nearly all her weight.

"I have these episodes too," Freckles says, and adds firmly, "Now, point me in the right direction."

She is insistent and Justine's legs feel like their bones have deserted them, so she does not object.

"I'm sorry," Freckles says after a while. "I wish I'd warned you it can be... intense. I've never figured out what to say. How to say it." She sighs.

"Not your fault. I can't..." Justine lets the sentence trail away. She cannot even talk about not talking about it.

"If your episodes are anything like mine, it will pass soon," the younger woman says. They still have not given each other their names, and Justine has no desire to. "I'm studying physiology. It's your body's reaction to stress. Like when you're already nervous and then a cat jumps out of the alleyway."

"I've been feeling like that since—" Justine stops herself, furious that she's nearly volunteered something no one else has a right to know.

They walk on in the unnatural stillness of the evening. "Yes," Freckles says. "Me too. Maybe—"

"Present your curfew passes," demands a voice from behind them. Both women tense and turn. A warden of the Watch, though he looks barely old enough to be out of his parents' house. Justine fishes her pass from her robe's pocket. She has not heard the nine bells, is almost certain they have not chimed. They are not out after curfew. A year ago, she might have made a fuss, but a year ago there had been no curfew, no riots, no Zara dead.

"Here you are, sir," she says, glad for once that her voice sounds tired, flat, not angry or despairing or any of a hundred other things. It sounds like nothing.

He examines it as though it is in code. Freckles still hasn't produced any documents. Belatedly, Justine realizes why. The other woman is an undergraduate and wouldn't have them. Tension radiates from her, but Justine does not understand it. She might face a fine, but has nothing more to fear—

Oh.

The warden looks up, first to Justine, then the other woman. "Curfew pass," he demands. Freckles' body is drawn taut as a warp. She stutters, reaching for words she doesn't have.

"She doesn't have them," Justine offers, though she has never been quick on her feet. Her escort's nails dig into her shoulder. "It's my fault, sir. I grew ill on campus, and she offered to help me get home. If she hadn't helped me out, she'd be home by now." Justine knows she should be afraid, lying to a warden, getting mixed up in who-knows-what. Her heart doesn't flutter. Earlier the flatness deserted her, and now here it is, returned for no reason she can name.

The warden's eyes move between them, then down to the sick on the front of Justine's robes. He sniffs the air, twists his face up like she is a refuse pile. "Where do you live?" he demands, and Justine gives him her address, two blocks away.

"And you?" Justine is certain Freckles will stumble again under his question, but she has gathered herself and gives him an address roughly halfway between Uni and Justine's flat.

"Get her home," he huffs. "And don't let me catch you out after curfew again." Justine feels him watching as they walk on.

She's been dreading her street, meaning to send her escort away before they near the lamp across from her flat. But now there is nothing to do but go forward.

If wishing made things so, the shadow would be gone, but it stands as it has the previous nights, silent and unflinching. She forces herself not to stare at it. "Come up," Justine says, half offer, half insistence. She can feel the other demurring. "The warden will be on the lookout for you."

That convinces her, and they stumble up the stairs to Justine's second storey flat. Freckles guides her to the sofa, and both sit heavily, their ragged breaths not enough to fill the silence.

Finally, Justine gets up to make tea, and when she returns, Freckles is shaking. Justine sits beside her, wraps her arm·around the younger woman.

"I'll be all right," the other woman says, clasping her shaking hands together. She rests her head on Justine's shoulder, takes deep, shuddering breaths.

Then it is over. Not all at once, but like a spring shower. You could not say when it stopped raining, precisely, but there comes a point when it clearly has. Freckles sits up, takes up the cup of tea Justine had placed before her.

"I'm sorry," Freckles says, breaking another silence after nursing her tea for some time. Justine turns back from the window, from her shadow.

"Twice you've apologized to me, twice it wasn't your fault. It's nothing."

"You saved me. You don't even realize—"

The walls are thin enough that Justine drops her voice. "You're one of them. The rioters."

The other woman stares at her like she's just sprouted wings. "Rioters? You mean the protestors?"

Justine does not understand. She sits beside Freckles, leaving space. She does not want to impose.

"But yes, I am," the younger woman continues, very quietly. "Part of them, I mean. Trying to support them. Most of the workers have much more at risk than I do."

Justine had felt the tightness in her acquaintance's body with the warden, felt her episode shake the sofa. She was already risking so much.

When the riots—the protests—started, Justine paid them little mind. Though they spilled out occasionally from the mill district, though there were curfews and further spikes in food prices that strained her and Zara's modest means, she knows little about them. No, that is not it. She has seen the hungry and homeless on the streets begging for scraps, read about the great machines in the mills that required fewer hands, heard whispers of the diseases that ran rife among the crowded flats of the millworkers. She knows people are desperate, but at first she had been too immersed in her studies to give it much thought. And later, there was nothing but grief.

She tries to avoid thinking about that day, but it was not the protestors who killed Zara. It was the Watch. The Watch who formed the line, who fired their muskets.

A surge of nausea hits her. She cannot speak of that, nor think of it. An ugly thought rises in its place. "And *Facing It Together* is, what? Recruitment?"

The other woman stands suddenly as if the seat—or Justine—has burned her. "What? No. Absolutely not." Her eyes are wide, her jaw tight. "It's for people who've lost their shadows. I can be passionate about more than one thing."

Is there nothing Justine can do well? She buries her head in her hands. After a few moments she feels weight beside her, a hand on her shoulder.

"I'm so—" Freckles pauses. "I shouldn't snap at you. It wasn't an unreasonable conclusion. Just an incorrect one. I invited you to the group only because I thought...I thought it might be of use. Like it has been for me."

Justine cannot look at her. "I don't know how to be passionate, not anymore."

Silence. Freckles stands, moves to the opposite wall, its dull stone face covered by a weave, just a simple thing, a two-color fractal in crimson and silver. Nothing more than an exercise, really, but Zara liked it.

"This is breathtaking," Freckles leans in to admire the detail. "I don't get to see many heartweaves up close. Your work?"

"Yes."

"Thank you for saving me back there," Freckles says. "Passion or not, without you I would have been doomed."

"If you hadn't helped me, you wouldn't have needed it."

"I had a twin, once." Freckles is framed by the weave, the dim lighting of the flat making her face an unreadable mask. "For a long time after, I couldn't...wouldn't reach out to anyone. I was terrified. Until I had to admit there were things I couldn't do alone."

Justine feels her awaiting a response, giving Justine space to form thoughts. But thoughts are the last thing she wants right now.

"I'll leave you be," her guest says. "Thank you for the tea."

Justine jumps up. In the tiny flat it only takes her a few steps to get to the door. "No," she says. "Don't go. Please." She is afraid she will be misunderstood, and more words rush out of her. "You can have the bed. I'll take the sofa. Too big a risk—to leave now."

She steps away, realizing she is blushing. She is just as inept at trying to signal that this isn't an approach as she ever was when actually trying to express interest.

The other woman looks at her curiously, as if trying to suss out what strings might be attached to the offer. "All right. But I'll take the sofa. I'm not going to kick you out of your own bed."

Justine winces. "I'd rather have the sofa," she says, and then, despite everything, it spills out. "I haven't been able to face the bed since, since..."

"I understand," Freckles says. "I'll take the bed. And be out of your way in the morning."

True to her word, she is up before dawn. Justine pretends to sleep as she slips out the door with first light.

Justine walks for hours. Down the narrow streets of the student district, as residents hurry to their classes, or congregate around carts selling pastries redolent of cardamom and squash. Here and there are shattered windows, iron gates slammed shut when before they would have opened to invite customers. Beggars, the ones willing to risk the Watch, ask for coin. She has none to give. Here and there, the Watch make their patrols, but without the urgency she saw last night. It is as though everyone has mutually agreed that during the day, things will carry on as if all is well.

But that is a fiction, a veneer. It is the artist's job to observe keenly, to see past the surface. As a Heartweaver, she learned to look beneath her own surface, until that well went dry, and when she attempted to pull raw material from her depths, not even dregs emerged.

What is beneath this surface? Lowered heads and few offered greetings. Windows shuttered when they should be thrown open, ready to catch the harbor breeze that will disperse the fog. Everything is gray, the color leached from the world. The people in the distance, mere shadows. Appalled, she looks away, anywhere but at the people. Above her, the familiar face of the neighborhood, her home for years now. Few people even put out their laundry these days, as if it would be stolen or used for torches or—she does not know what. The few pieces that remain hang limp in the damp air, yellow towels and sheets the only splash of color in the near-monochrome morning.

The blocks pass under her feet. She moves with neither urgency nor direction, but when she realizes where her legs are taking her, it feels inevitable. The stone fronts of the student district give way to the newer neighborhoods abutting the mills—rickety timber buildings, occasionally reinforced with brick, that were thrown up when the mills opened, as people flooded in from the country for the jobs they offered. Now there are few jobs, worse wages, more hunger. Now there are burned-out buildings and violent confrontations with the Watch. Now there are loved ones dead in the streets.

She arrives at a block like any other, some of its buildings standing, many partially burned and collapsed. One might miss it entirely, save for the twine with which the Watch cordoned it, the signs demanding everyone keep out. No one seems to be on guard, though, and the four small shrines are evidence people have been ignoring the command. Justine glances around, then slips under the barrier. Not really a barrier, just a line that is easy to cross, once you know you can.

The shrines are arranged in a semicircle. Artists' likenesses of the four victims stand in each shrine's center. Piles of tiny objects cluster around them: candles; small gifts; tear-stained notes; a series of small, smooth rocks stacked into piles; bundles of yellow wildflowers.

Justine cannot bring herself to look at Zara's picture and does not need to. She can bring Zara's face to mind as easy as breathing, but is not eager to invite that pain into herself. The others, though, she stares at. Strangers, all of them, two younger and one older. All protesters. She found she could no longer think of them as rioters. And even if they had been, it was the Watch who struck them down. Who murdered them, she at last lets herself admit. The Watch, who left Zara bleeding on the street, when all she'd been trying to do was take food to her cousin. Yes, it was the Watch who did it. Not the protesters. Not the millworkers and the jobless, not students like Freckles.

That's when she notices: these shrines are new, as yet untouched by rain. They're piled atop ash, the same ash that darkens the brick wall behind them, effacing, what? She steps closer. A chalk-drawn mural, its details lost now, charred beyond recognition.

So that was why the protests had gained renewed strength. Someone had tried to destroy this memorial. Very recently. Someone wished to erase the dead. Justine staggers, kneels before the shrines. The hollowness in her chest remains, but now it is not alone. It shares space with rage.

Some time later she finally forces herself to rise, feeling eyes on her from the dark facings of the buildings across the way. She turns to see movement around a small bonfire inside one of the damaged structures, its front wall collapsed, its beams charred and bent. There are people in its depths, watching her, their shadows—

—no, not only their shadows. Severed shadows are there too, moving on their own, with no people to cast them. Humans and independent shadows both, living in the wreckage. She has never seen anything like it, had no idea shadows gathered, or that there were people who might share space with them. Lives, even.

She yearns to go speak to them, to understand, to ask why her shadow is haunting her. But she hesitates. This is their home, and she is an outsider here. They have not approached her and have allowed her to pay her respects. She will not intrude. She wants to leave an offering at the shrine, but her pockets are empty save for her curfew pass. She has nothing to offer.

Justine wanders on. The fog turns to drizzle as she drifts among streets, through alleyways and unfamiliar districts. Desperate times make for desperate people, and it is unwise to walk alone through neighborhoods she does not know. She does not care, cannot imagine going to campus and her loom, and is not ready yet to turn towards home. When she realizes what she is waiting for, her fists clench, her spine tightens like a thread stretched too far, ready to snap.

She walks until it is full dark and raining in earnest. The wind has at last arrived, a gale blowing in from the harbor, pelting the streets with a nearly-horizontal

downpour that brings in the autumn cold for the first time
this season. Her teeth chatter. She pulls her arms around
herself. Cold does not matter. Nothing does.

Time to face her shadow.

It waits for her, its body made somehow even less
substantial by the wind passing through it in gusts. It
shimmers like a reflection on a lake's surface. Justine
thinks it turns to her as she approaches, but it is hard to be
certain.

She trudges toward it. She can neither make herself
hurry the confrontation nor run from it. When she
reaches the edge of the pool of lamplight, she hesitates, her
momentum at last failing her.

"You *are* mine," she says at last. There is no doubting
it, the shape, the posture, even the blurred edges atop its
head where her hair will never truly cooperate, will frizz
up at every opportunity. She realizes she's been hoping
to be wrong, that it would be someone else's shadow,
someone else's problem. No such luck.

The shadow, being a shadow, says nothing.

"I'm here," she says. "I know you've been waiting for
me, and I'm here. What do you want?"

No sound but the rain, no movement save for a slight
tilt of its head, a mannerism Zara teased her about, one
that always meant she was struggling with a puzzle, a
challenging weave or a difficult exam question.

"You shouldn't be here," Justine says, hating its silence,
the staccato of her heart's pumping, the rain's drumbeat.
"I never wanted to be without you, but I can't change
things. They killed her, and you tore away and now..."
Justine trails off. Now what? She cannot put things right.
She once saw another student, furious with his own weave,
take a pair of scissors to it. The heartweave had torn
easily, as if in rebuke of the effort that had created it. All
that remained were frayed threads on the ground. No
going back.

"I can't do anything for you!" She realizes her voice is rising, becoming a scream. It feels like the sound comes from someone else's lips. She has found her rage, but still she is nothing but a passenger to it. "I don't know what you want, and I have nothing to give. It's over. Don't you understand?"

The shadow folds its arms across its chest.

"I can't help you! I can't help either of us!" She shouts and the shadow wavers, though whether through reluctance or under a gust of wind-blown rain, she cannot say. "If you won't show me what you want, then go. Just go. Please."

The shadow tilts its head, and that is all. So much time bracing herself to confront it, and she is no better off than she was before. No, that is not quite true. She is not afraid of it anymore, just bone-tired.

She turns her back on the shadow, rapidly crosses the street, her shoes sloshing with water. Her shaking hands struggle with the lock. When she finally opens the door, she hesitates, turns around.

"If you're not going to leave," she shouts across the street, "then I suppose you'd better come inside."

The shadow doesn't move, but by the time she ignites the lamps in her flat, it is there, standing in the corner by the sagging bookshelf. It does not move while she strips out of her wet robes, starts her kettle boiling, and waits to stop shivering. It is there when she goes to sleep, and still there in the morning.

FOR THE NEXT few days, Justine worries she will wake with the shadow's hands around her throat, or with it trying to stitch itself to her skin, or some other horror. But it stays in the corner, makes no effort to approach her, to communicate. It only stands.

She goes onto campus repeatedly but can draw no
essence for her work. Finally, she abandons her geometric
exercise and begins sketching a new project.

The threads come fitfully, sometimes flowing like they
once had, other times drying up completely, and most
often a trickle that Justine hopes is more akin to priming a
pump than a well on its dregs. She can think of nothing to
do but keep at it, for at least she is working again. Nothing
is repaired, but at least she is weaving again.

She is several days into her new project and not
quite halfway through when Professor Morinth enters
unannounced. He stares at her work on the loom, woven
in gleaming yellow, with two somewhat abstracted faces.
She doubts he has been to the shrine, doubts he knows
these faces, but the meaning of the yellow weave is clear.
It's the color hung from windows, left to dangle from
clotheslines, the color adopted by the protesters. There is
no mistaking her intent.

Of all the arts faculty, Morinth is the one who might
have been sympathetic to this new direction, this rejection
of the meaninglessness of art, and she can see in his eyes
that he is. For all the good it does her.

"I have no choice but to report this," he says after
a long silence. "You know it will bring an end to your
studies here."

Pain flares through her, white-hot, the kind she has not
felt since her early days of mourning. This is all she has
left and now he is taking it away too.

"You do have a choice," she says, more sharply than
she intends. "We all do."

He stares at the loom. Even half-finished, there is no
denying the work's politics, and she wouldn't do so even if
she could.

"It's lovely," he says, as though the aesthetics are what
is at issue. "But the university will never allow it. It can't
seem to be taking sides."

She should fight this, demand to finish her project unmolested. Champion her rights as an academic. But she suspects that he will put neither the university nor himself at risk. And without his support, she can never hope to finish, never hope to pursue a career here or at any other university. Even if she wins the argument, she loses everything.

"If you won't stand up for your students' right to make the art that calls to them—" she says, and hates herself for the generality. "If you won't defend me, then what use is any of this?"

He has never looked younger, standing with his mouth agape. "We can forget about this," he says at last. "Finish a more...practicum-appropriate project, earn your doctorate, and then you're free to pursue whatever projects you wish."

Such a tempting offer. How she craves continued access to a loom, the credential she's worked so hard to earn, the comfort and security of life behind a university's walls. The loss of her stipend means even her frugal lifestyle will exhaust her remaining funds before long, and then where will she be? Out on the streets? Begging her mother's estranged family for a place to sleep? Another jobless worker, and one without useful skills?

She stares at the vivid yellows pulled from her essence, the intricate images she has never previously managed. Of what use is the promise of someday completing her work if it can't serve its purpose now, when people are grieving? What use is her art if it cannot offer them even this small thing?

"If I can't do the work I need to do," she says, "then what's the use of this place?" She begins removing her work from the loom, carefully tying off ends, even though she knows she will never be able to finish it.

"The university does so much good," he says, even now unwilling to look at her. "It provides safety, stability, and essential funding to the city. There's no need to get... irrational. No need to burn everything down."

A terrible choice of words: she is not interested in destruction, but in creating something new. And now she is certain that, whatever he once was, he is a functionary, a cog, driven to defend that thing which molded him to its needs. He has allowed himself to see his highest goal as protecting it. As though the ivy-bound walls were going anywhere, with or without his protection.

She carefully folds away her project and tucks it under her arm. "Goodbye, Professor," she says.

Justine is almost out the door when he calls out to her. "Don't throw this all away, Justine," he says, breaking decorum by referring to her by her given name. When she turns back to him, incredulous, he meets her eyes for just a moment, then looks down. "Don't take this so personally."

"It's not personal at all. I see that now." She leaves him standing there. At the edge of campus, she hurls away her robe. It catches briefly in the wind, tumbles and snags on a hedgerow that marks the place where the university ends and the streets begin. She walks home in loose trousers and overshirt, only the half-finished wall hanging under her arm and the slip of paper in her pocket remaining as markers of the dream she leaves behind.

JUSTINE RETURNS TO the cellar, to Freckles and the others. If the group finds it odd that she has returned after her rushed exit from the last meeting, no one says so. Only Freckles raises an eyebrow, studying Justine's face for a moment, then looking behind her to the stairway, as if she expects someone else to enter. But Justine is the last, and they begin as they had before with the invocation of their rules.

Others speak occasionally in that room bound by silences, by absence. Justine does her best to listen, but her heart is beating loudly in her ears. When she finally summons the courage to speak, her voice sounds strange. It isn't, as before, as if she is looking at herself over her shoulder, but still she feels she does not fully know this person whose words she hears.

"My shadow stands in the corner of my flat." She pauses, expecting, what? Shock or surprise or disbelief. And she finds something like that on some faces, but by no means all. The leader—no, she realizes, the facilitator— only nods. "It had been watching my flat from across the street. I invited it in."

She falls silent, glad to have unburdened herself but not feeling the relief she hoped for.

"How do you feel about it?" the facilitator says after a few moments.

"I want to know what it wants." Justine hears in her own words something like petulance. There are a couple of nods, but the facilitator only quirks an eyebrow, as if waiting. Justine hasn't answered her question.

"I don't know how I feel. I was afraid of it, but now I just...wish it would tell me why it is here. Or go away and leave me in peace."

"Where would it go?" Freckles asks. The facilitator looks in her direction but doesn't interject.

"I don't know," Justine says. "Wherever it wants. To live with other shadows, maybe." She feels some of the air leave the room. One of the others, a younger man, flushes. The facilitator lifts her hands, palms down, as if doing so will calm everyone.

"They do what they will," she says. "Some do go join communities with other shadows, or stay with their people, if we'll let them. My own shadow visits me once, maybe twice a year."

Justine blinks, trying to make sense of this. "What does it want?" she asks at last, and the woman shrugs.

"They keep their own counsel. But I like to think it just wants to see how I am getting on." When Justine has nothing more to say, she continues. "They are no different than we are, getting by without us as best they can."

She smiles at the young man who reacted so strongly to Justine's words. "Would you like to tell us about how it goes with your shadow?"

He nods, takes a deep breath. "It's splitting. Becoming two shadows." He pauses for a long time before continuing. "It's strange to feel it moving on without me. Like if I'd shed a limb, and it had grown a body, started its own family."

Justine came here hoping for answers, for reasons. Theorizing, as always. As though reasoning could change the fact that she'd lost Zara, then been sundered by grief. As though answers could heal her. Foolish.

After the meeting, she approaches Freckles, worried she is violating some unspoken taboo. But she needs to do this.

"Would you...would you be willing to stop by my flat sometime?" she asks. "I have something I'd like you to see."

To her surprise, Freckles nods at once. "Of course. I'll come tonight, if that's okay." Seeing Justine's worry, she adds quickly, "I, uh, acquired some papers after last time."

They make it to the flat without incident. Only when Justine brings up the lights does she realize her shadow isn't in the corner. She gasps. "It's gone."

"More likely it's still on its way. It followed you to our meeting. Did you know that?"

Surprised, Justine shakes her head. "It never has before, that I know of."

Freckles takes a seat on the couch, and sure enough the shadow passes through the wall and takes up its spot in the corner. "I visit mine occasionally," she says. "It's hard to communicate with them, but from what I can tell it works with new shadows, helps them get...situated, I suppose." She smiles. "They have their own places, their own means of mutual support."

Justine had never seen anything like that before the shrine.

Then again, why would she? People with shadows would rather talk about anything than those without, and she had never walked those neighborhoods, never taken herself down streets where those who aren't welcome find means to survive.

She sets about making them tea again.

"My name is Mina."

"Justine." She responds without a thought, surprised at herself. Well, it would be ridiculous to carry on without names, and she couldn't very well share her project with a stranger. "I should have asked before, but I wasn't ready."

"It's nothing," Mina says, smiling. "There's no rush. Only what you're ready for." Justine feels suddenly warm.

They drink their tea and speak softly. Justine tells Mina a little about Zara, about the errand of kindness she was on when she died. She isn't ready to share the details, but she sees Mina understands. It's a comfort to have someone to share experiences with, but also tense, as though any wrong move could pressure an exposed nerve.

"Well," she says at last. "I meant to finish this, then figure out what to do with it. But now I know it won't be finished, and, um, it seemed right to show it to you."

She unfurls the half-completed weave, lays it down on the floor in front of Mina. The pair of faces, the victims of the Watch's weapons, are impressionistic; Justine's memory and technique weren't up to the challenge of composing realistic portraits from memory, but she thinks she captured something of their essences as displayed in the shrines, some sense of them. She's refrained from making visual reference to the futures they would never have. No one needs such reminders. This was to be a tribute, not a funeral shroud.

She was saving Zara for last, but that will never come to pass, now.

"It's gorgeous," Mina says, very softly, wiping at her eyes.

"I'd meant to leave it near the shrines, for people to do with what they wanted," Justine says. "But then I thought it wasn't my right...and now it doesn't matter. I've lost access to my loom."

Mina pulls a tissue from her robes, blows her nose. "They kicked you out for this, didn't they?"

"Yes. I just thought...maybe you would know someone who might have some use for it." She rolls it back up carefully, and when she looks up, Mina pats the sofa beside her.

"I can do better than that," she says and reaches out to take Justine's hand.

§

THEY SLIP THROUGH a series of narrow alleyways, switching back and watching for any sign they are being followed. When Mina is certain they are not, she stands before a nondescript door, knocks twice, then thrice more. An older woman admits them and bolts the door before she turns to greet them, and shakes Justine's hand. Her grip is firm, her hands calloused, her smile inviting as cool water.

"Mina told me what they did to your project," she says. "I'm so sorry. My name's Raye."

"Justine. It was going to happen sooner or later. Thank you for having me."

Raye clicks her tongue. "There's no need to thank me. This space is for mutual aid."

As Justine's eyes adjust to the darkness of the expansive room, she can see what Raye means. It must have been a warehouse, once, its high ceiling lost in darkness, pools of lamplight marking various stations. In a nearby one, a pair of adolescents work to lay out a newspaper. Other stations seem to hold murals or images in progress. At one, an elderly person, stooped and alert, cuts lengths of cloth into bandages.

"It's amazing," she says. "I've never seen anything like it." Never even imagined it.

"You haven't seen anything, yet," Raye says, and takes her to the loom.

It is set off behind walls, unlike most of the other stations, to allow for the indirect lighting that is best for weaving. It has none of the majesty of the Grand Loom, nor even the straightforward functionality of the tertiaries. It is stranger than either and to Justine's eyes far more impressive. The word that springs to mind is *wild*. It seems to have been assembled out of scavenged pieces of broken looms, supplemented with parts reclaimed from other projects. Where the looms she has seen before were clearly purpose-built, this one is a kludge, a monument to tenacity. Someone, or many someones, who were never meant to heartweave, have found a way.

"It's glorious," Justine says softly, reaching out to touch it as she would a holy relic.

"My child is our expert," Raye says. "But the Watch have them locked up, who knows where. It's only right that it be used."

"Thank you," Justine wipes at her eyes. "I will do my best to honor them in their absence."

Raye smiles, clasps a hand to Justine's shoulder. "Everyone who works for the cause honors it."

It takes time to secure the weave to the loom, which lacks the extreme precision of the tertiary looms. On anything but a heartloom, resuming the project in this way would have been impossible, and even on a heartloom it requires many hours and great care. For once, Justine does not theorize about the arcane forces that govern the heartloom. Theory does not matter. What matters is the work, the patterns of her feet on the treadles, the shuttles gliding across the shed. The harness Justine wears is a bit small for her, uncomfortable, and even now the thread will not always come.

When it will not, she wanders, taking in other projects, speaking to their crafters, to Raye, or to Mina, when she is present.

When the thread does emerge, she works ceaselessly, afraid of the next dry spell. Some nights she sleeps on the floor of the shared workspace, others she returns to her apartment, knowing she can no longer afford it, but not yet prepared to leave behind its absences. Her shadow joins her in neither location, though she watches for it. It has gone as inexplicably as it had returned.

The weave is nearing completion when Raye stops by to admire it. Her smile is still kind, but there is something else in her face, something determined.

"What do you plan for this when it is finished?" she asks.

Justine tells her what she hoped, and why she hesitated. It is not her place, not her right.

"Don't you have as much a right as any of us to mourn the dead?" Raye says.

"But I wasn't involved. I didn't join when I should have. I was lost in my own dreams, and then my grief." Justine turns away, fighting back sobs.

"You're here now," Raye's voice is gentle. "Are you ready to do the work?"

Justine is.

"Good," Raye says. "Then I know a way you can help."

THE PROTESTORS CHOOSE Royal Way, one of the widest streets in the city, for the march, and Raye has made it clear to Justine that she should keep an eye on side roads. Sooner or later, the Watch will move to close them off, and then it will be time to get clear as quickly as possible. Justine is terrified, and Mina has repeatedly assured her she doesn't have to participate. But Justine has spent weeks in the craft space, finishing her project, helping others with theirs, sharing meals and stories, wine and regrets.

Marching with the protesters won't put back together what was severed, will never mend the hole in her life where Zara had been. It is no cure. But it is a small thing she can do to help. Like her heartweave, now draped from a long pole, carried aloft by Mina, by Justine, by friends and strangers.

She is terrified, even as the crowd fills in, even as their combined presence ensures that whatever fate awaits them, they won't face it alone. There is no certainty, no easy answers. Nothing left but to put one foot in front of the other.

The Watch are still assembling themselves as the protesters begin their procession, more joining their number all the time. Up the Royal Way they march, shouting slogans demanding food, justice for the fallen, an end to the Watch's violence. Justine's voice is fragile as cracked glass, but it rises with the others.

A collective gasp goes up the marchers, a sudden movement in the crowd. Justine tenses, expecting the furious report of musket fire. And then she sees them, joining as a group: shadows. Dozens of them, maybe hundreds, slip into the crowd, take up positions among the other marchers. Ripples of nervous energy shiver through the protestors, through Justine. Her own shadow is there, not beside her, but not far away, either, one among many. She nods to it, and it inclines its head, then nods in return. There are so many shadows, each one the result of a pain so great it ruptured someone's life. Yet here they are.

Amidst the throng, it's hard to tell the severed shadows from those still attached. Under the yellow tribute banner Justine wove, the protesters advance. Shoulder to shoulder, they march into their uncertain future.

Acknowledgements

THIS COLLECTION WOULD never have existed without the kindness, wisdom, and support of many people.

My parents taught me that reading was among life's greatest joys. Their love and support have never wavered, even when I kept choosing paths practically designed to give them anxiety. It's a gift to count my siblings among my dearest friends, despite my terrible babysitting and worse puns.

My editor, dave ring, believed in my work even when I didn't, and told me hard truths when I needed to hear them.

I've been blessed to work with many generous and supportive teachers, including Thomas Fox Averill, Pat Cadigan, Lisa D. Chavez, John Chu, Marisa P. Clark, Andy Duncan, Amy Fleury, Daryl Gregory, Kij Johnson, Daniel José Older, Daniel Mueller, and Connie Willis. Without the staff and faculty who made possible the University of Kansas's summer science fiction classes, I would never have started down this path.

My beloved Clarion West class of 2017 have sustained me through difficult times, shared joys and sorrows, provided insight, and encouraged me to be the best version of myself. Much love, Team Eclipse!

Neile Graham, M. Huw Evans, and the staff and volunteers at Clarion West changed my life in the best possible way.

Drafts of these stories were cultivated and pruned by many people, including Phoebe Barton, Andrea Martinez Corbin, and Natalia Theodoridou.

Between them, A. T. Greenblatt, Iori Kusano, Alexandra Manglis, Vina Jie-Min Prasad, Adam Shannon, and Emma Törzs provided brilliant insight on every story in this collection.

The queer speculative fiction community is amazing, and I could never hope to give back even a small fraction of what they've done for me. R.B. Lemberg and Bogi Takács were beyond generous with friendship, food, conversation, and wisdom. They entered my life at the exact moment I needed them, and before I realized how much I did. Charlie Jane Anders and Annalee Newitz took me under their wings when I knew no one and understood even less. Susan Jane Bigelow provided mentorship, friendship, and kind, patient guidance. Sarah Pinsker was the reason I started writing speculative fiction, and one of the first people to make me feel at home here. Dozens of other queer folks were there for me when I needed them, and I can only hope to pass on a fraction of the generosity that was gifted me.

So many friends have been there to provide love and support during awful times. Sarah E. Azizi, Michelle P. Baca, Iris Bristol, Tommy Grice, Lisa Hase-Jackson, Jonathan Bohr Heinan, Gary Jackson, Juan J. Morales, Ian Schmidt, and Bart Sprague have all been there when it meant everything.

My therapist, Dr. Peg McCarthy, continues to help me make sense of things.

Grace and Yasi showed me the trail and helped me walk it.

Many trans folks and radicals have fought, bled, suffered, and — more often than some people want us to remember — triumphed. They're my ancestors, as surely as anyone who shares my DNA, and without their work, I could never have survived.

My spouse, Nora E. Derrington, has been my biggest cheerleader, most trusted advisor, and favorite person for many years. All this despite so many dad jokes. (The punchline is apparent, Liz. Get it?)

Story Notes

ALL THE HOMETOWNS YOU CAN'T STAY AWAY FROM

I was born and raised in Topeka, and when I left for graduate school, I swore I'd never live there again. Four years later I returned for a job, and I've been here ever since. I lived on Mayo Avenue for years, and if you're ever on the south side of town, odds are good you'll smell the racoons-in-a-gym stench, too. (Thank the Frito-Lay plant, and never look at chips the same way again.) In this reality, they tore down the state hospital building years ago. Other realities remain frustratingly out of my reach.

I have a fondness for small details in stories, the ones that may not matter to anyone but me. In this story, that detail is the street names at the beginning and ending.

THEIR EYES LIKE DEAD LAMPS

This is the oldest story in the collection. I wrote the first draft in 2015 and it wracked up an impressive list of rejections before *Lady Churchill's* bought it. While its subject matter and setting are unusual for me, I like to think it contains a number of my obsessions. In particular, I love stories where the strangeness never resolves into easy answers. Rivers are long, mysterious, and ever-changing, after all.

Unplaces: An Atlas of Non-Existence

"Unplaces" owes tremendous debts to Jorge Luis Borges and Theodora Goss. Goss's "Cimmeria: From the Journal of Imaginary Anthropology" is referenced directly here. It borrows its structural conceit from the masterful "Ogres of East Africa" by Sofia Samatar. The inclusion of Penglai was based on a suggestion by Iori Kusano.

Every writer, I suspect, has pieces they love more than their audience does, and this is one of those for me. It's my earliest queer anti-fascist story, and reflects my love of including references to non-existent books in my work. One of my fondest wishes is that other authors will make reference to my not-actually-existing books in their own work.

The Good Mothers' Home for Wayward Girls

I wrote this at Clarion West 2017. My week 5 story, it began as an experiment in using the first person plural in a story. It's always been very important to me that the Thing Outside The Walls is a real threat. The Good Mothers are genuine in their desire to protect the girls, though their treatment is perhaps worse than the disease. Sometimes a revolt is necessary, but we can't ever be sure the outcome will be favorable.

Requiem Without Sound

I am among the least musically-talented people ever born, so naturally I'm obsessed with music. This story's version of the requiem mass is abbreviated, but so far no one has complained about the missing sections.

Because I enjoy experimental structures, I often set myself challenges to write stories that break "rules." I don't think anyone has ever remarked on it, but this story features only two characters. They never directly interact, and their lives never overlap.

Lyndsie Manusos included this story in a list of "15 Science Fiction Short Stories to Take You Out of This World," along with works by Ursula K. Le Guin, Octavia Butler, Charlie Jane Anders, N. K. Jemisin, and others. I'll never stop being thrilled to have somehow been included on a list with such titans.

DEAD AT THE FEET OF A GOD

I wrote this story in early 2020, a result of having been thinking a lot about radicalization and the necessity of resistance. Facing the horrific prospect of another four years (at least) of a Trump presidency, I struggled to imagine how we would defeat the authoritarians who were gaining and entrenching power across the world. I still struggle to imagine it.

I can't recall if the story's structure or themes emerged first, but from the early planning stages of this story I found them to be inseparable. Radicalization isn't inherently good or bad. What we are radicalized against and into makes a great deal of difference. One can be radicalized into QAnon or religious fundamentalism as surely as one can be radicalized against fascism.

Increasingly, I suspect that my work will always return to the question of how we should respond to neo-fascism, climate change, hierarchies, and other existential threats. In that sense, this story's answer is taken directly from Ta-Nehisi Coates: "...resistance must be its own reward, since resistance, at least within the lifespan of the resistors, almost always fails."

If asked, I don't have anything like definitive answers about what we should do to save each other. But the necessity of resisting evil remains.

CASE OF THE SOANE MUSEUM THEFTS

The Soane Museum is very real, and if you're going to visit any museum in London, it's the one I'd most recommend. An architectural marvel, it features an eclectic and fascinating collection, one gathered by Sir John Soane, and left to the state rather than his estranged son. It is exactly as problematic as you'd expect from a collection gathered by a rich man during the depths of the British Empire.

We must empty museums of looted artifacts, and the massive resistance to that idea is further proof of how urgently it is needed.

These characters insist that I return to them someday.

THE CRAFTER AT THE WEB'S HEART

This began as a theoretical discussion at Clarion West: how can one build a second-world fantasy at short story length? Traverse and its absent spider-god arose from my attempt to answer that question. The magic system is my response to the idea that all magic must have a cost. While I've seen this story draw comparisons to a certain comic-book hero, for me this story isn't a superhero's origin: it's an apotheosis.

Despite Danae not being explicitly trans, this is perhaps the most trans story I've written.

HOPPER IN THE FRYING PAN

Science fiction doesn't predict the future, as Ursula K. Le
Guin famously argued. This story is as close as I've ever
come to writing predictive near-future SF. I don't mean
"block-chain will collapse, leading to a re-centralizing
of personal information." I mean that our lives will be
increasingly controlled by big data and surveillance (by
governments and private companies), in the service of
keeping us consuming and compliant. To say that barely
counts as extrapolation.

BLADES, STONES, AND THE WEIGHT OF CENTURIES

This is the third of three (so far) tales set in the world I
first explored in "The Crafter at the Web's Heart." The
other, "The Vixen, With Death Pursuing," appeared
in *Maiden, Mother, and Chrone*. This story exists because I
believe, as Laura Jane Grace sings, "we can be the bands
that we want to hear." I'd add: we should write the sword
lesbian stories we want to see in the world.

THE GRASS BOWS DOWN, THE PILGRIMS WALK LIGHTLY

I struggled for years with this story, and repeatedly
abandoned partial drafts of it. The structure and
emotional beats to make it cohere arrived at Clarion West
(there's a theme here: those six weeks were by far the most
creatively rewarding of my life). Readers I admire were
and are divided on whether the Odin's ravens sections are
worthwhile. I leave that for the reader to judge. Certainly
they are key to how I think of this story.

◊

FIVE REASONS FOR THE SIGN ABOVE HER DOOR, ONE OF THEM UNSPOKEN

After this story was published, I realized some readers were interpreting its trans themes in ways very different than I intended. I believe that a work speaks for itself, and once it is out in the world, the author loses any right to dictate how it should be read. But because I wanted cis readers to understand what the story means to me, I wrote a blog post about it. At the urging of Robert Minto, I include that blog post here:

I AM INVISIBLE: TRANS COMMUNITIES AND THE CIS GAZE

I have a new story out in Abyss & Apex, *about trans bodies, trans communities, and responding to the cis gaze. [...]*

I can't talk about ["Five Reasons"...] without talking about what it means to be a trans woman viewed constantly through the eyes of cis people. In many ways I am lucky, in that I am about as close to invisible as a trans woman can be. I don't mean that I pass, exactly, but that I am white, fat, middle-aged, and not conventionally attractive. I'm also privileged in that my transness isn't immediately obvious to everyone who sees me.

I am, in short, the kind of person who goes unseen: a white woman who men don't desire.

And yet on occasion a tweet of mine will go viral, and with it will inevitably come men sliding into my DMs eager to chat me up. I don't engage with them, but their presence signals a particular kind of interest. They want me, but they want me because I'm trans, because they imagine they know what my body must be like. This is gross, of course, but early in my transition it was also strangely affirming: straight men wanted to fuck me. What is a more fundamental experience of womanhood than that?

My tastes don't generally run toward men, for which I am extremely grateful, for how could I ever know if it was me they desired, or if I was only an object to fetishize?

I am invisible. Except when I'm getting death threats. Except when I'm catcalled. Except when I put on my cutest dress and thick eyeliner and am called 'sir.' Except in the way I can't meet strangers' eyes in restrooms. Except when I am an object of desire or contempt.

Even when I am invisible, the threat of the cis gaze follows me everywhere. Transmisogyny shapes my interactions, even with people who are neither transphobic nor misogynist.

I wrote this story to respond to the voyeurism of the cis gaze, but also to explore the spaces trans folks make for each other, the bits of ground in which we see, support, and protect one another. The spaces where we can hold each other (apart)/(up)/(together).

Such spaces are the other half of my story, spaces where I am neither invisible nor objectified. Spaces where I am seen.

The cis gaze is monstrous, but trans communities are beautiful.

EVERYTHING THE SEA TAKES, IT RETURNS

This started, as much of my work has, from a prompt by Alexandra Manglis, who is a Wizard of Writing Prompts, her power unmatched. I've never lived near the sea, and I hope that isn't too painfully clear here.

I'm often told that anarchism is naive and/or dangerous, and that it isn't viable at any kind of scale or in practice. I concede that may well be the case, and offer only this counterpoint: look at where hierarchies and coercion have led us. I am not optimistic for the future of humanity, but if our species is going to survive the next couple hundred years, we'll need better models than the ones we have been following.

My fiction has been accused of being didactic, and to the extent that my radicalism, queerness, and anti-fascism are central themes, I suppose I agree. But I don't set out to *instruct* anyone. I see my work as groping towards tentative answers to big questions. Maybe that's why I identify so strongly with these characters: nothing is certain, most especially our futures. But the struggle remains.

SHADOWS OF THE HUNGRY, THE BROKEN, THE TRANSFORMED
My day job is as a professor, and perhaps some of my feelings about the nature of academic institutions come through in this story. At times I've been counseled to avoid being seen to push back too aggressively against what I see as injustices at my school, since I don't have tenure. I've seen what happens when people keep quiet in order to gain power, telling themselves that they will be able to do more good once they accumulate more institutional clout. It isn't pretty.

May my loyalty always be to people over institutions, with those who suffer over those who are comfortable. And when I fail at that, I hope people who care about me will call me out.

As for the shadows, there is no explaining them: they exist. Trauma may cause them to be separated from their human, but they are not a metaphor.

Publication History

The author would like to acknowledge the following publications where these stories first appeared, sometimes in slightly different forms.

"All the Hometowns You Can't Stay Away From"

Fireside

"The Crafter at the Web's Heart"

Apex

"Dead at the Feet of a God"

Beneath Ceaseless Skies

"Everything the Sea Takes, it Returns"

Lightspeed

"Five Reasons for the Sign Above Her Door, One of
Them Unspoken"

Abyss & Apex

"The Good Mothers' Home for Wayward Girls"

PseudoPod

"The Grass Bows Down, the Pilgrims Walk Lightly"

Analog

"Hopper in the Frying Pan"

GlitterShip

"Requiem Without Sound"

EscapePod

"Shadows of the Hungry, the Broken, the Transformed"

Cossmass Infinities

"Their Eyes Like Dead Lamps"

Lady Churchill's Rosebud Wristlet

"Unplaces: An Atlas of Non-Existence"

Clarkesworld

About the Author

Izzy Wasserstein is a queer and trans writer of fiction and poetry. Her most recent poetry collection is *When Creation Falls* (Meadowlark Books, 2018). She teaches writing, literature, and film at a public university in the American Midwest and shares a home with the writer Nora E. Derrington and their animal companions.

About the Press

Neon Hemlock is a Washington, DC-based small press publishing speculative fiction, rad zines and queer chapbooks. We punctuate our titles with oracle decks, occult ephemera and literary candles. Publishers Weekly once called us "the apex of queer speculative fiction publishing" and we're still beaming. Learn more about us at neonhemlock.com and on Twitter at @neonhemlock.